ACTUAL REALITY

CAT MANTRA

First published in Great Britain in 2016 by

The Book Guild Ltd
9 Priory Business Park
Wistow Road, Kibworth
Leicestershire, LE8 0RX
Freephone: 0800 999 2982
www.bookguild.co.uk
Email: info@bookguild.co.uk
Twitter: @bookguild

Copyright © 2016 Cat Mantra

The right of Cat Mantra to be identified as the author of this
work has been asserted by him in accordance with the
Copyright, Design and Patents Act 1988.

All rights reserved. No part of this publication may be
reproduced, transmitted, or stored in a retrieval system, in any form or by any means,
without permission in writing from the publisher, nor be otherwise circulated in
any form of binding or cover other than that in which it is published and without
a similar condition being imposed on the subsequent purchaser.

This work is entirely fictitious and bears no resemblance to any persons living or dead.

Typeset in Palatino

Printed by TJ International, Padstow, Cornwall, UK

ISBN 978 1 910878 36 1

British Library Cataloguing in Publication Data.

A catalogue record for this book is available from the British Library.

For my son, Joshua

PART I
GENESIS

Chapter 1

It was a warm summer morning, the sunshine peeking through the curtains. Josh Mantra's eyes blinked open. Half a second later he was sat bolt upright in bed.

'It's my birthday!' he said to his Bart Simpson poster, 'I'm twelve!' He looked at the clock on his Harry Potter sticker-encrusted bedside cabinet. 'Hmm, 5.52 am,' he said out loud, 'that'll do!'

Much like any 12-year-old, the odds on Josh waiting a moment longer to go and check on the birthday present situation were *astronomical*! And sure enough, within seconds he was out of bed and scurrying downstairs in his – now a little bit too small – Pokemon pyjamas. He didn't like Pokemon any more, or at least as far as any of his school-friends knew.

As he rounded the end of the banister his heart began to pound. The huge pile of presents in the centre of the living room was crowned by what he had wished and prayed for: a gleaming brand new computer!

'*Yeeeeeesss!*' Josh shouted, and he ran back upstairs, jumped on his mom Katrina's bed and woke her up with a huge hug and a great big smacker on the cheek.

'Mmmf?' said Trina as she squinted out of the corner of her eye at him.

'Thanks, Mom, you got me my computer!'

'Actually it's off me *and* your dad. We had to club together, those things don't come cheap you know!'

Before she knew what was going on Josh had

disappeared again, leaving the word 'Wow!' trailing behind him.

An hour later, Trina made it downstairs, still a little groggy and hankering after her morning cup of coffee. She was confronted with a mass of wrapping paper, and after digging her way to the middle, finally found the gleeful Josh carefully piling and sorting his plethora of gifts.

'Wow!' he said again.

'Is that the only word left in your vocab, dear?' Trina asked jokingly as she futilely attempted to locate the kitchen door.

'You wouldn't believe it, Mom, I've got six new PlayStation games, two James Bond DVDs, two Simpsons DVDs, a skateboard, and the new Aston Villa kit off Nan!'

'What about the nice packet of socks off your granny?' said Trina.

'Oh yeah,' the incredibly over excited voice replied, 'and them as well! Can we set my computer up now Mom?'

'Give me a chance to wake up, darling,' said Trina as she finally located the kettle.

Josh knew this probably meant coffee, bath, breakfast, more coffee. So he put on his new Villa kit and settled down to watch *The Simpsons*.

Another two hours later, still only 9 am – and on a Sunday – they had carried all the various pieces, monitor, keyboard, speakers, printer, etcetera up to his room, and he was all set up and ready to go.

'OK, son, I'll leave you to it then, I'm just going to read in my room for a while,' said Trina, which roughly translated meant 'go back to bed for a couple of hours'. 'Oh! One last thing, your dad told me to give this to you last.' She retrieved an untidily wrapped, cube-shaped object, roughly 8 inches across, and passed it to Josh.

'Cool! Another present!'

Josh laughed at his dad's present-wrapping ability, Dad was great at playing *Goldeneye* on the Nintendo, but he couldn't wrap up a present in a month of Sundays! This was mainly due to his impatience; Dad liked to get on with things, and found sitting cutting bits of paper to shape and trying to stick them neatly with Sellotape both boring and annoying.

He stared at his last birthday gift. 'I wonder what it could be?' Addressing Bart again now: 'Oh well, no point in sitting here wondering, let's find out!'

For one last time (until Christmas that is!) he gleefully tore at some wrapping paper, and was finally presented with a note, and a box containing a Blu-Ray ROM disc, and a very odd-looking gizmo to attach to his PC. It looked kind of like a large red crystal, which somehow levitated above its black base from which the lead to attach it to the computer extended. On the box it said in bold letters, 'ACTUAL REALITY'.

Josh opened the note: 'Dear Josh-dude, handle this piece of equipment with care, it will bring you many amazing adventures. Love, Dad XX.'

Chapter 2

Josh had attached the AR (Actual Reality) Unit to the PC, rebooted, and was ready to go.

'Mom, I'm hungry can I have some lunch?' he shouted (it was now 10.13!). No reply. 'Oh well, I can wait,' he said as he dropped the Blu-Ray ROM into place. He grabbed hold of the mouse and eagerly clicked the 'Install' button, and moments later his computer's disc drive started to whizz.

'Wow.' Josh's favourite word of the day was whispered this time, as the red crystal on the AR unit began to glow. Just a dim but entrancing light in the centre at first, soon replaced by an incredibly bright and enchanting light. Suddenly the red lights were streaking out of the crystal and searching the room, feeling for something, quite what, Josh didn't know. He soon found out. The moment one of the strands of light touched him the rest of them were on him. Wrapping him up, encapsulating him. But it wasn't scary, it was amazing.

And seconds later he wasn't in his room any more, he was sitting in an Aston Martin DB5 – just like James Bond's!

'Wow!' For a few moments Josh sat, stunned (as one would!). As the car sped through luscious green hillsides, the sun blazing from a virtually cloudless sky, he began to take in his surroundings. The incredible red leather upholstery in the Aston, the many gauges in the dashboard, the satellite navigation system, the weapons systems, his dad sitting in the driver's seat wearing a perfectly pressed tuxedo. *Whaaaaa?!*

His Dad sitting in the driver's seat, wearing a perfectly pressed tuxedo. He had to keep going over that last bit. His Dad sitting in the driver's seat wearing a perfectly pressed tuxedo ... his Dad sit-

'Hiya Josh!'

Josh snapped back to the land of ... wherever he was.

'Dad? What the doof is going on?!'

Josh's dad lifted his shades and turned to look at him. 'I never told you about my other job, did I?'

'You mean ... you're James Bond?!' Josh had lost control of his jaw and was now incapable of closing his mouth.

'No, Josh, James Bond doesn't really exist. I created this scenario to make you feel comfortable.'

'Wow!'

For the next two hours they cruised through mountain highways, and then down along twisting coastal roads, and during this time Josh learnt a lot of things he never knew before about his dad:

1. He worked as a law-keeper, and an emergency rescue officer.
2. He had worked in a thousand different realities, via the AR.
3. His superiors, elected governors of the Inter-Dimensional Federation (basically, the law keepers of everything – ever), had chosen Josh as his successor.

They pulled up on a high cliff-top, facing out onto an almost unbelievably blue ocean.

'So basically, Josh, after searching thousands of dimensions, in myriad universes, the only suitable successor they have found is *you*. I know you are still very young, kid, and don't worry, I'm gonna be around for a long time yet to help you out. So are you up for it?'

'Am I ever, Dad! I am gonna rock!' Josh was quite into his new calling.

'OK, kid, you've just got to pass the three final tests.'

As Josh began to reply, he noticed his Dad's finger moving swiftly towards the button marked 'Ejector Seat'.

'Dad? What three final te-*aaaaaaaaAAAAAAA*!' As he tried to speak the final word of his sentence, the roof blew off the Aston Martin and Josh was suddenly catapulted high into the air.

Flying out over the sea, he looked down and caught a glimpse of the silver Aston Martin. He could just hear his Dad shout, 'See ya later, Kidda!'

Josh's momentum slowed, and for a moment he was stationary, almost floating. Then he was falling, faster and faster, plummeting towards the ... racing track? Seconds later he landed softly in the seat of a shining red Ferrari Formula One racing car, which was, according to the speedometer, travelling at 210 mph!

His helmet radio crackled (where the helmet had come from he didn't know), and his dad's voice came over the speaker. 'Test number one, Josh: reaction times.'

Although Josh barely had time to even register what was happening, he quickly focused on his task, timing the corners perfectly, accelerating out of the chicane, cruising past other competing cars with ease. Just over a minute later he completed the lap, and took the chequered flag.

Another voice came over the radio, this time he didn't know the voice, it was sharp, and digital. 'Test number 1 completed successfully, 98 percent.'

But Josh had no time to relax and enjoy his victory, because the cockpit of his F1 car had already begun to melt, and in its place, another cockpit grew, that of a *Starfighter*.

Now the radio in his slightly altered helmet was silent, just for a while, giving Josh the chance to acclimatise to his new situation. Flying through the depths of space in a one-man fighter, incredible views surrounded him: stars, planets, huge flowing nebulas.

'Awesome,' was the only word that could describe it. His gloved hands were resting on the control stick, and he noticed two buttons easily reached by his thumbs atop. 'Hmm.' As he pressed them, brilliant white beams shot from the laser cannons on the wings of his fighter. All the hours his mom claimed he had 'wasted' on his PlayStation were paying off now! In a way, he almost felt like he had done this before.

And then the oasis of calm was over as the radio once more crackled into life. It was the digital voice again, 'Test number two: targeting and coordination.'

'I wonder what the doof that means?' Josh thought to himself, and then, in the distance ahead he could see something. Or rather, some things. A great deal of things! He was headed straight into an asteroid field! Momentarily he was surrounded by thousands of huge lumps of rock and iron, tumbling aimlessly through the infinite void.

Like a seasoned expert he manoeuvred his ship through the field, swooping close to the larger asteroids, blasting the smaller ones with his lasers. The next five minutes seemed like a lifetime, as time and again Josh avoided collision by the tiniest of margins.

Just as it seemed the field was thinning out, a robotic voice started shouting at him: 'Proximity alert! Proximity alert!' Josh glanced down at the scanner in the control console. A black hole off the starboard bow!

'Oh boy!' shouted Josh as he slammed the control stick hard to the left, simultaneously hitting the booster rockets, hoping that the extra acceleration would throw him clear of the huge gravity well surrounding the black hole.

And then he had made it. The sleek little ship was

clear and once more gliding gracefully through empty space. And without a scratch on its silver hull.

The digital voice was in his ear, 'Test number two completed successfully. Score: 99 per cent.' And everything went red.

Chapter 3

Josh was home, sitting in his computer chair as if he had never left. He looked around his room, his gaze finally resting on Bart Simpson. 'Did that actually happen? What happened to test number three?'

Then it dawned on him that he had probably been gone for hours and his mom would be worried sick, so he checked the clock. Still 10.13. 'Wow!'

Much like a few hours ago, he ran into his mom's room excitedly. 'Mom, Mom, you'll never guess what I've been doing!'

'Hmmf?' His mom had disappeared without trace under a 13 tog quilt! The one-eyed squint was also back as her head emerged from the comfy bedspread. 'What have you been doing then, darling?'

'Erm ... nothing much. Shall we go and watch my James Bond DVD?'

He didn't really know why he hadn't told his mom about his amazing adventure, but he decided to keep it secret for now.

The rest of the day was much like any birthday: lots of visits from relatives, more presents, loads of crisps, sweets and pizza, but Josh couldn't help thinking about that morning. Was it real? Maybe he had just fallen asleep at his computer. By the time his mom tucked him in that night, he was tired out and ready for a good night's sleep.

Trina gave him a kiss on the forehead. 'Goodnight Josh.'

He gave her a cheeky wink, 'Night, Mom. Can I have an Xbox for Christmas?'

She smiled. 'We'll have to see about that one, dear!' And with that she turned off the light and clicked the door shut.

Josh curled up and closed his eyes, but he could still sense the red glow that had filled his room even through his eyelids. He knew as he opened his eyes again that the light was from the AR unit, but what he didn't expect to find was that it was transmitting a holographic image of his dad, sitting on the end of the bed.

'Well done, kid, you scored exactly the same as I did when I joined the company.'

'Dad! So it *was* real!' Josh jumped up to give his dad a hug, but fell straight through the projected image and off the bed.

'I'm not *actually* here right now Josh, I'm a hologram.' Josh's dad said with a wink.

'Of course, of course! I'm just too excited, Dad! But, but what happened to the third test?'

'You've already passed that one, son – when you didn't tell your mom. It's a pain I'm afraid but nobody on this planet can know about our occupations. Now then, are you still happy to be a part of this, because I can easily tell the bosses that you want to stick to being a normal kid, you know?'

'Yes, Dad! I so want to do it!'

Josh's dad laughed. 'I thought you might say that. OK, well in the time to come you are going to experience many different realities, many different dimensions in time and space. One day you might be fighting dragons, the next you might be a master wizard. And I know that wherever you are you will do your best. We might even get to work together on some missions. And if you ever need me, the IDF (Inter-Dimensional Federation) will call me. Well, sweet dreams, kid.'

The image of Josh's father began to fade. 'Dad! Wait!' Josh shouted. The image snapped back into focus.

'Yes?'

'How will I know when they need me?'

'Oh, yeah, sorry Josh! Under your pillow you'll find a remote for the AR unit, kind of like a pager. It'll alert you when you need to be here.'

'Great! Night, Dad!'

'Night, son. Sweet dreams.'

'Who needs dreams when I've got Actual Reality!'

Josh's dad had a knowing smile on his face as he faded from view. The room finally went dark.

Josh got back into bed and, as he lay down, reached under his pillow to feel for the AR remote. For a moment he began to worry as it seemed not to be there, but then he felt the cool crystal against his hand. He grabbed it and pulled it out to have a look.

As he opened his hand, he noticed it fitted nicely into his palm. It was a perfect miniature of the AR crystal, and in the centre he could see a tiny red glow. As he looked closer he could see that it wasn't just a light, but an image, a perfect, crystal-clear image of the galaxy, millions upon millions of stars rotating around each other. It was almost hypnotic. Josh closed his palm once more around the crystal, and then closed his eyes too. As his tiredness crept up on him, he could only think of one thing to whisper before he slept: 'Wow!'

PART II
COLONEL CAVEMAN

PART II

COLONEL CAVEMAN

Chapter 4

It had been about three weeks since his birthday, three weeks of adjustment for Josh. Adjusting to knowing his new purpose, knowing what he would be doing with his life. It was a bit early to have made that decision. Up until just under a month ago he was undecided between rock star, spy or kick-boxing world champion. Or a combination of all three. Of course now he was certain that at some point he really *would* be all three! He just didn't know what dimension it would be in!

He had received a letter from his dad a week ago, letting him know about the remuneration side of his new job as 'Defender of the Known Universe' as he liked to think of it. He hadn't even thought about it, getting paid for doing all the amazing things he would be doing. But he had always wanted to be rich as well. Turned out he wouldn't be rich rich. The government would wonder where all the money had come from. But he would be OK. And he would be able to look after his mom as well. That meant a lot to him.

As things were, it was 3.52 pm on a sunny afternoon in July, and Josh was walking home from school with friend and wannabe girlfriend Stacey.

'What are you doing now, Josh? Do you want to come to mine?' she said, with a hopeful glint in her eye.

'I dunno,' Josh replied half-heartedly, his thoughts suddenly dragged back to this world. 'Maybe. I could text Mom, I suppose. What will we do?'

'We could play my Hobbit board game, except I don't like it cos you always beat me.'

'Erm … OK then. What the doof?! Oh hang on, my phone.' Josh usually kept his phone on silent vibrate so it didn't get confiscated in class. He pulled it out of his school trouser pocket and checked the display to see who it was. 'Strange,' he said, 'no one there.'

Then his pocket vibrated again. '*Huh*?!' He reached back in, and pulled out the AR remote! The palm size crystal was glowing bright red, and when he looked closer he could see words somehow forming from within: 'EMERGENCY – ATTEND AR UNIT'. This was it! His first real mission.

'What's that?' Stacey was staring at the AR remote, looking more than puzzled.

'I'm sorry, Stacey, I have to go,' said Josh as he started to increase his pace.

'But Josh! What about the game? What is that thing?!' Her last words were not heard as Josh was now running at full pelt for home.

'See you tomorrow at school!' he shouted over his shoulder as he rounded the corner into his street.

'Hrumph! Fine! I didn't want you to come anyway,' said Stacey. No one heard her. Well, maybe a lamp-post.

Josh was home within moments. He had to calm himself for a second as the excitement was stopping him from being able to actually get the key in the door! Then it was in. He clicked the latch back and bounded through the kitchen, through the lounge and up the stairs to his room.

The words 'Hello Josh, how was school?' chased him, but never caught up.

'Come on come on,' he said impatiently as he waited for the PC to boot up. It was a brand new P7, state of the art, but still seemed to take forever. As soon as the hard drive had stopped clicking he simply pressed the only button on the AR remote, and the AR unit came to life. As before, the red strands of light streaked from the crystal, and eventually enveloped him. And his adventure had begun.

Chapter 5

Josh was sitting in a very futuristic-looking room, with chrome tables, very plush chairs with keypads that did who knows what on them, and a large screen at the front of the room said simply 'IDF' in large red letters. The room seemed to be lit by long blue tubes which stretched along all the walls.

Then a door wooshed open behind him and his dad walked in. 'Hiya, kid!'

'Dad!' Josh said excitedly. And then immediately tried to calm himself down.

'It's OK, son, I know you're gonna be hyped up for your first mission.'

Josh's dad (known to grownups as Cat, Cat Mantra) strolled round and sat on the corner of a desk at the front of the room.

'OK Josh, we haven't got much time, this is the situation. A pre-industrial colony on Praxis 4 (an Earth-like planet in a parallel dimension) is being terrorised by a vicious carnivorous reptile, nearest Earth comparison: Jurassic period.'

At which point Josh had to interrupt. 'Erm, Dad ... I'm a kid! Can you speak in kid talk, please!'

'Oh sorry Kidda. Basically, a dinosaur. Something like the size and with the appetite of a Tyrannosaurus rex.'

At this point Josh's usually olive complexion had gone somewhat pale. 'A T-Rex?! My first mission and I have to fight a T-Rex dad?! I was thinking more along the lines of a bit more motor racing, or ...'

'Josh! We haven't got time to discuss it, those people are in danger.'

Josh knew when to shut up. But he went a little paler all the same.

'Now. I'm going to issue you with the standard IDF interface, which you can use to contact base at any time. And of course if you need emergency evacuation. It also has a voice-activated computer interface, and will be loaded with all the data we have on your mission parameters.'

He tapped a few buttons on the chair next to him, and what looked like a watch materialised on Josh's desk. Josh's dad walked over and picked it up. He crouched by Josh and looked him in the eye as he picked the interface up and strapped it to his wrist. 'Its called T.A.T.E., or Tate, short for Tactical And Territorial Evaluation.' He gently rested a hand on Josh's shoulder and said, 'Don't worry, son, I know you must be scared, but I also know you can do this. Are you ready?'

'I don't know, Dad ...', Josh took a deep breath and stood up. He looked his dad straight in the eye. 'Yes. I am.'

He could see the pride in his dad's eyes now as he said, 'Computer!' An electronic beep emanated from ... somewhere. 'Activate Transport.' Josh watched the room fade away as he was enveloped once more in the now familiar red lights.

ZZZZZZZZZAP!

And then he was there. Praxis 4. Wherever the doof that was. He was standing in a small clearing, surrounded by tall tropical trees. It was warm, and it was raining. But a refreshing kind of rain, the kind you get when it's been baking hot sunshine for a few days.

Josh looked down at what he was wearing, and immediately uttered his usual exclamation: 'What the doof?!' His feet were wrapped in some kind of animal hide, bound tightly with a primitive form of twine. He had more animal hide tied crudely about his person, and he soon realised that his right hand contained a large wooden club!

Then he heard a distant rumbling. And voices shouting, sounding panicked. They were coming closer, and fast. He could also hear splintering wood, and the thrashing of foliage being torn ruthlessly down. Then suddenly a group of about 15 cavemen burst into the far side of the clearing, running straight at him.

The leader was calling out to him, 'Oogalaboogala! Oogalaboogala!' Josh didn't have a clue what that meant, but the man seemed to get more and more agitated as they approached. 'Oogalaboogala! Oogalaboogala!'

Josh didn't know if they were planning to attack him, but they didn't look angry, they looked scared stiff. Then suddenly a huge tree in the forest disappeared from view, crying out with a loud *crack*!

'That can't be good,' Josh thought out loud.

'Oogalaboogala!' shouted all 15 cavemen this time.

Then the Tate interface beeped, it looked oddly out of place now on his arm.

He looked at the screen, it was saying, 'Translation mode?'

The cavemen were almost on him now, and he was starting to panic himself. 'Yes!' he shouted, and this time as the cavemen swept past him, nearly knocking him over he understood them: 'Run!'

And then he knew why. Now emerging at the far side of the clearance was the monster. It was almost as tall as the trees themselves, and it was moving towards him at an incredible speed. Before you could say 'Actual Reality' Josh was on the heels of his now fellow cavemen, hoping the caves were very near.

Chapter 6

They soon managed to reach safety, and Josh then spent the night with the cavepeople, hearing stories of how the dinosaur had terrorised them for some time, and how they feared for their children. All their animals had been killed, and their crops were trodden down and ruined; soon they would also have no food.

As the fires burned low, and the people settled down to sleep on beds made of twigs and leaves, a little girl approached Josh, holding a doll fashioned from what looked like more animal hide. 'Please help us,' she said, and then she walked back over to her mother, and curled up to sleep.

At least she's safe here in the cave, Josh thought. And soon enough he too was sleeping.

Josh was awoken just as the first beams of sunlight spread through the entrance of the cave. Not by his now fellow cavepeople, but by Tate. And with a subtle beep.

He looked down at the screen on the piece of equipment that didn't quite fit in with his pre-civilisation look. It was saying 'Activate voice mode?'

Josh wasn't quite sure how to respond to this in his early waking moments, so simply mumbled, 'Er, yes?'

'Good morning, Joshua,' said Tate, in a very frank and digital way.

'Er …' (again). 'Hello, Tate, I didn't know you could talk!' came Josh's now awoken reply.

Tate was swift in his response. 'Joshua, I am a fully voice-activated and vocal response unit. I am programmed to aid you in any way possible on your missions for the IDF.'

'Great!' said Josh, before realising he should keep his voice down to avoid awaking the people close by. And in a more hushed tone, 'What can I do, Tate? This is my first mission, and I am, to be honest, scared stiff!'

Tate's calming tone actually helped Josh to relax a bit. 'This reptile, or dinosaur as you will think of it, is out of time Joshua.'

'What do you mean, Tate?'

'In essence, Josh, it has fallen through time. These creatures were actually extinct on this planet many years ago. This particular one, has fallen through a singularity which at its centre had created a time warp.'

'Oh my gosh, Tate! What can we do?' asked Josh, whilst still containing his excitement and, yes, his fear.

'I can contact IDF to re-establish the singularity, Joshua. Your job is to make sure the creature walks, or runs, through it.'

'So, I have to set a trap?' asked Josh, looking at Tate (who now had an interesting, friendly face on his watch face).

'Yes, Joshua. And you must leave me on the ground at the centre of the trap. Don't worry, I won't be gone. Well, I *will* be gone, back to IDF. And I'll see you on the next mission.'

'OK, Tate, I got it.'

At this point, the little girl who had spoken to Josh before crawled up to his shoulder. 'Who are you talking to, Josh?'

Arrgh! Josh was startled. 'Er, no one, just myself!'

'But I heard a voice calling you Josh!'

'Well, erm …' Josh was trying to find a way out of this, but gave up and changed the subject. 'What's your name?' he enquired. (Thankfully, the translation achieved by Tate was still in operation.)

'My name is Esetomi,' she replied, with a gleeful look in her eyes. 'I like you, Josh!'

'Esetomi, I need to speak to your mom and dad,' said Josh. 'I have a plan.'

Soon after (32 minutes, 47.895 seconds according to Tate), the sun, and the entire tribe, had risen: 15 cavemen, 15 cavewomen and 9 children. Some were washing in the sea, some were lighting a fire for breakfast, and the children were running around joyously. Josh also took joy in the fact that this small tribe of people could carry on as normal despite the huge monster on their door (or perhaps cave) step.

And he was intrigued to discover from Tate that they actually saw him as a full-grown man! Josh was projected in different forms to suit his surroundings. Dad forgot to tell him about that bit.

At breakfast (which was very nice fish, but without batter and chips, unfortunately!) Josh told the tribe of his plan. All day they would stay in the cave, and be quiet. *Then.* On the evening they would have a *party*?! Right in front of the cave. With fires and many tribal drums. The cave was at the top of a gully surrounded by sandbanks, perfect for Josh's plan. The bait for the trap was, and had to be, the tribe itself.

Many of the tribesmen were wary of Josh's plan, and indeed of Josh. But his relationship (although short-lived so far) with Esetomi, and how much she had taken to him, had endeared him to her father, Agabolo. Fortunately for both Josh and the tribe, he was the Chief.

Agabolo approached Josh and said, 'We don't know you, outsider, but we know we are safe in our home.' (The cave.) 'If you can rid us of this monster, we will be forever in your debt.'

Josh needed to say nothing. The plan was set. They awaited dusk in the cave, which was well lit with flaming torches. Some of the children wanted to go and play outside, but Josh taught them games within the cave, such as 'Hide and Seek'. They loved it!

And come sunset, the trap was set. There was one huge central fire, two more beyond it. (Tate had informed Josh that the dinosaurs of Praxis 4 did not fear fire. It attracted them, just as light does a moth.) And four drummers made a *big* noise on instruments fashioned from hollowed-out trees with animal skins stretched tightly across them. The tribespeople danced around the fire. It really was a party; however, it was staged, and they danced and drummed, in fear of the monster.

The children had been told to stay in the cave, but they peeked out at the incredible feast of sound and vision in front of them, not knowing why they weren't allowed to join in. Agabolo sat on a huge chair, almost a throne, made from what Josh could see was branches, bones, straw and twine. (Or at least in Earth terms it was.) He kept a watchful eye on all the proceedings, and made sure the children stayed inside.

And then Josh heard a different beat.

Much deeper.

And then another.

On the third he noticed a branch in the fire fall, and cinders fly into the air, such was the vibration through the ground.

The people felt it too, but they kept on drumming and dancing, just as Josh had asked.

And then that beat got faster.

And faster.

It almost fell in time with the drummers as the 50 foot tall creature ran along the beach towards their little gully.

And then it was there in front of them! As it skidded sideways to turn towards them from the shoreline. A towering dinosaur, mouth gaping, and teeth bigger than Josh.

At this moment, Esetomi shrieked from the edge of the cave, 'My Dolly!'

And she ran, straight past her dad, and the drummers, and the dancers, and the fire!

Her lovely little toy was lying on the sand, about 50 yards past the fire.

'Stop, Esetomi!' cried Josh, but she was away and running. Josh had no choice, he gave chase. At every moment the huge dinosaur got closer, Esetomi got closer to her beloved Dolly, and Josh got closer to Esetomi.

Josh quickly realised he wasn't going to catch her up in time, so at the last moment, he ripped Tate off his arm, and threw him forward as far as he could. Tate landed next to Dolly, Esetomi reached down for Dolly, the monster's gaping mouth closed in on Esetomi.

Josh shouted, 'Activate!'

Suddenly, a huge whirlpool appeared behind the dinosaur. A whirlpool in the air. And the creature was picked up, and spun into the vortex. (With a *whoooosh!*)

And all was silent. The drums had stopped as the cave people watched aghast.

Esetomi picked up Dolly, and looked at Josh. She didn't seem to realise what had just happened. 'I got Dolly! Thank you, Josh!'

As the red wisps of light encapsulated Josh, he heard the drums begin again, and the chants of the tribes people. 'Josh-u-a, Josh-u-a!'

ZZZZZZZZZZAP!

And Josh was gone.

And Josh was home.

IDF log Supplemental

The next day Josh rushed home from school because his IDF remote had informed him he had an email waiting.

Upon booting up his computer he was surprised and amused to find that the email was from 'Inter_dimensional_federation@yahoo.com'. Josh sniggered at the 'Earthbound' email address.

The message read thus:

To: Kidda
From: Daddio

Hey Kidda, I've heard all about your first mission, well done. You nailed it! (I knew you would of course, it's in the blood!) ;-)

Close one at the end, but sometimes that's what it's all about, snatching victory from the jaws (literally in this case) of defeat.

Yeah, I forgot to tell you about the age projection system. The IDF will project you, as you, at an age suitable for your environment. In this case, the cave people would not have taken advice from a 12-year-old kid, so you looked 25! And this is done using your DNA coding. So you were actually you, at 25.

Bonkers isn't it?!

But never forget, Kidda, this is not a game. The people you help are *real*. And if you get hurt on a mission, *you* get hurt. Your projection in *actual reality* cannot protect your mind from the shock you will feel. And a feedback loop caused by the injury to your projection would cause you *real* harm.

Make maximum use of Tate, Kidda. He's your greatest ally on any given mission. He's certainly gotten me through a scrape or ten!

OK. That's it from me for now. Take care, son, and I'll see you soon.

Lotsa love, Daddio.

Josh sat back in his chair with just one thought, 'Wow!'

PART III
AHOY CAPTAIN JOSH!

PART III

Chapter 8 IDF briefing

Location: Planet Earth.
Situation: Three kids: Emma, age 14, Aless, age 4, and Jake, age 6. Whilst spending a weekend on their uncle's boat, find themselves lost at sea. Their uncle had gone ashore to fetch supplies when a fog fell on the anchored vessel. When the fog lifted, they found they had lost their mooring, and drifted out to sea.
Josh Projection Age: 12.
Mission Objective: Get them back to safe harbour.

Chapter 9 Lost at sea

ZZZZZZZZZAP!

'Here I go again!' thought Josh (out loud as usual). The next thing he knew he had materialised on a yacht! And opposite him in the cockpit were three stunned and frightened faces. It was dark, but calm. And the boat was bobbing gently in the quiet waters. No lights or sign of land could be seen.

'Hey, gang, I'm Josh, and I'm here to help,' was the first thing Josh could think of to say.

'But ... where ...?' stuttered Emma.

'How ... ?' questioned Aless.

'Flippin 'eck!' exclaimed young Jake.

Emma, who was sitting in the middle, arms protectively wrapped around her younger siblings, managed to form a whole sentence next. 'We were just sitting here, and then ... you appeared in a swirl of red light.'

'It was scary,' said little Aless.

'No it wasn't, it was cool!' exclaimed Jake.

'I can't explain,' Josh continued, 'I can only tell you I was sent here to help you.'

Josh got up and had a look around the boat. It looked about the same size as one he had sailed once with his dad, and the sails and rigging looked similar too. 'That's a break,' thought Josh (not out loud for once). 'I might just be able to sail this thing.'

'Well ...' Emma was stuttering again, 'w-what do we do now?'

Josh realised his new friends were still very scared, and he needed to try and make them feel confident that all would be OK.

'First things first, Emma, why don't you make some warm milk for Aless and Jake, it's past their bed time! And while you're doing that, we'll make a plan.'

'H-how did you know our names?'

Now Jake was stuttering too! 'It was all in my mission briefing Jakester, there's more than just the Big Guy watching over you now!'

'Alllright!' said Emma, already perking up. 'Let's do it!' And she disappeared below. Moments later the cabin lit up and she started getting busy sorting out a pan to warm some milk.

Josh noticed that the wind was starting to pick up, and thought, 'Great. This would be a good time to get under way then.' He clicked the button on his Tate 'watch'. The screen lit up with a glow which, although it was blue, still seemed warm. And the satisfying computerised beep emanated simultaneously.

'Hey, Tate!' said Josh. He still couldn't help but get excited at the truly unbelievable incredible-ness of his life now.

'Good evening, Joshua,' replied the watch. Tate had been programmed to speak with the Queen's English (kind of posh, like the butler in *Batman*). And somehow, it seemed to suit him.

A moment after Tate spoke, both Aless and Jake catapulted excitedly into the cabin shouting, 'Emma! Emma! His watch talks!'

Josh smiled to himself. The kids were relaxing. Good. 'Tate, give me our current location.'

'Location unavailable.'

'Erm ... what?'

'Location unavailable, sorry Joshua.'

'Why the doof is that, Tate?' (There has to be a hitch huh?!)

'Due to atmospheric disturbance I cannot connect with any global positioning satellites.'

Josh sat and thought for a moment. And as he thought, he noticed that the yacht's navigational lights had sprung into life. Emma was sorting what she could.

'OK, Tate, how about connecting with the IDF mainframe?'

Tate emitted his beep. Moments later: 'Unfortunately Joshua, due to an electrical storm all outside communication is down. Emergency evac is, however, functional.'

'Well, Tate, we're not going anywhere without them. We'll have to do it the old-fashioned way. Can you be a compass?!'

'Of course I can, young Josh.' And with a trusty beep, the points of the compass appeared on the watch-face of Tate. N, E, S, W, all in that 'warm' blue.

'Emma!' shouted Josh. 'Where were you anchored before your uncle went ashore?'

'Cawsand!' her voice came back from below decks. 'It's across the water from Plymouth.'

'Right,' thought Josh, 'we have to head North-North-West.' Tate could easily have navigated via the stars, but there were none to be seen tonight.

Josh immediately set to unfurling the foresail, and moments later the wind took it, and Josh heaved on the tiller to pull them on course.

'I'm going to need a hand raising the mainsail,' said Josh, which was immediately followed by a yelp of excitement from little Jake in the cabin. He stumbled up the stairs shouting, 'I'll do it Josh!'

'You're not quite big enough, Jake,' Josh replied,

pleased that the little ones were now more excited than scared. 'You keep a look out for me, while your big sister helps me with the sail.'

'Aye aye *sir*!' shouted Jake.

'Your milk's ready, Jake,' Emma's voice drifted up into the cockpit.

'I want to drink it out here, Emma, I'm on lookout. Pleeeeease!'

'It's OK, Emma,' said Josh. 'Ensign Jake is doing a grand job. I doubt he'll sleep yet.'

At which young Aless jumped out into the cockpit shouting, 'Me too!'

Emma emerged from the cabin, being careful not to spill the warm milk from the cups, looking a little disgruntled. Josh sensed her anxiety and said, 'Don't worry, Emma, it's all hands on deck!'

Aless and Jake took their drinks and seemed very happy to have them. Jake making sure he kept to his lookout duties, although there was nothing to be seen.

Josh noticed Aless look up at him in the faint light spreading up from the cabin. 'If Jake is Ensign Jake, what am I?' she asked, looking both cute and puzzled.

'You are Yeoman Aless,' Josh replied, 'in charge of looking after both Ensign Jake, and First Mate Emma.'

She grinned at him ecstatically. 'And Captain Josh!' she stated with confidence. Satisfied, she returned to sipping her milk.

Now Josh and Emma could focus on the task in hand. Emma had obviously helped her uncle out before as she had the cover off the mainsail and stowed in a matter of minutes. Josh wrapped the mainsail halyard around the winch and shouted 'Heave!' as they began to hoist. At first it was easy, but the last couple of feet seemed to take an age and a *lot* of energy.

And then it was done.

Chapter 10 The storm before the calm

'What's she called, First Mate?' asked Josh.
'*Anastasia*,' Emma replied.
'She's beautiful. Just like my dad's first boat.' And as he said it, *Anastasia* was settling nicely under full sail on the NNW heading Josh had chosen.

Of course, Josh couldn't be sure this was the heading he needed, but at least he *was* sure he was heading back towards the English coast! He glanced at Tate; the compass dial told him he was spot on.

'Tate, what's our speed?'
'Seven knots, Joshua,' replied Tate, the watch.

Josh was pleased at this, and they sailed on for two hours without need to tack. During this time Aless and Jake nodded off and Emma carried them below decks and got them into their bunks. Their bunks were in the forepeak (right at the front) of the boat, and very secure. As it turned out, they needed to be.

At 2 am local AR time, the wind started to pick up. And up. And up. Josh at first was pleased, as their speed picked up. 8 knots, 10 knots, 12 knots. Too much.

Emma screamed in fright as a wave broke over the bow.
'Don't worry Emma, hold on tight!' shouted Josh as he tied a rope to her buckled-on life jacket. The rope was secured to the boat. 'You're not going anywhere without me and *Anastasia*!'

Gusts rattled the rigging, and water poured over the deck into the cockpit. Josh was having trouble holding onto the tiller, but he didn't want Emma to see a moment of doubt in his eyes.

Josh knew he must reduce sail: 'I have to reef!' he shouted through the wind, and as he said it, a huge gust pushed the boat so far over that Josh could not see the sky, but only sea. He heaved *Anastasia* round to face the wind. And as the wild water splashed into his face he shouted to Emma, 'Release the Genoa sheet!'

Emma turned and swiftly undid the rope holding the large foresail close-hauled. She let go as the wind pulled it from her hands.

Josh furled the sail in seconds. He was in automatic mode now. 'Thank God Daddio showed me the ropes,' he thought. He pulled *Anastasia* back on course, under just the mainsail now. And that was plenty.

'Current speed 7 knots, well done, Joshua,' came the pleasing calm words from Tate.

Chapter 11 Land-ho!

The storm continued for what seemed to be forever, but was in fact only an hour. All of a sudden, it passed. Just like that. Gone. As were the clouds.

The stars were twinkling across the horizon, and *Anastasia* was gently gliding through the water.

A very relieved and very tired Emma beamed at Josh. 'Thank you so much, Josh, that was *amazing*.'

'A cuppa would go down very nicely right now, First Mate.' replied Josh with a wink.

As Emma rushed below decks to check on Aless and Jake, and put the kettle on, Josh glanced at Tate. He was surprised to see a '☺' smiley on the watch face. Beep!

'Location calculated via Astral navigation, Joshua,' said Tate. 'Your course prediction was correct, we are currently 5.3 nautical miles from Cawsand Bay.'

Josh couldn't contain his jubilation. '*Yeeeesssssssssss*!' he shouted as he jumped into the air (avoiding the boom below the mainsail of course!) 'You're nearly home First Mate!'

Soon, as the first light of dawn began to break, all four of the *Anastasia* crew were in the cockpit, drinking tea and scoffing the toast that Emma had rustled up.

Aless and Jake had both, incredibly, slept straight through the storm.

'I'm back on watch, Skipper,' said Jake. 'Did I miss anything?'

'Nothing at all,' Josh replied as he and Emma looked knowingly at each other. 'Smooth sailing.'

About an hour later, the sun was up, sparkling on the peaks of the waves. The quiet breeze was pushing them (now back under full sail) gently forward, and Ensign Jake had spotted the Cornwall coast long before. First Mate Emma was holding the tiller, as Josh was on kettle duty this time.

This time it was Yeoman Aless who shouted up, 'What's that?!'

Josh popped his head out of the cabin to have a look. There was something in the water, virtually directly ahead. As they sailed closer, they could make out that it was a rowing boat, out past Plymouth breakwater. And soon they could hear cries of 'Ahoy!'

The entire crew shouted back 'Ahoy!' and moments later Emma, Jake and Aless knew exactly who was in the dinghy. They jumped up in excitement and all at once shouted '*Unnnccle*' Yes, it was their uncle, who had set out at first light in the vague hope that he would spot them.

Josh brought *Anastasia* close to the rowing boat, and shouted 'Heave to!' as he expertly came alongside and turned the yacht into the breeze. Emma grabbed the painter (the dinghy's rope) and tied it on. Then she helped her dad clamber aboard.

All his kids grabbed him for a massive family hug and kisses all round. Then they all looked at Josh.

The children's dad said, 'Thank you so much for this. But, who are you?'

And as Aless shouted 'I love you Captain Josh!' ...

ZZZZZZZZZZAP!

And Josh was gone.

And Josh was home.

PART IV

SUPERSONIC BLACK HOLE

PART IV

SUPERSONIC BLACK HOLE

Chapter 12 IDF briefing

Location: Black hole on the edge of our galaxy.
Year: 2177.
Situation: The giant passenger ship *Aquarius* en route to Earth Colony Vega XII is in *big* trouble. The entire crew and all passengers are stuck in hyper-sleep (a system used in the 22nd century during long voyages). After an attack by IDE patrols (the Inter-Dimensional Empire), the ship's computer suffered major damage, and failed to awaken the crew and alter course. Leaving the *Aquarius*, and all aboard, on course for certain destruction.
Crew Complement: 589.
Passenger Complement: 12,500.
Josh Projection Age: 12.
Mission Objective: Save the ship!

Chapter 13 Blazing through space

ZZZZZZZZZZZAP!

Josh was aboard the *Aquarius*. He quickly took in his surroundings, not very palatial. A huge steel-coloured room, packed with containers and low-lit. He had materialised in the centre, and 100 metres in front of him he could see a large grey door. It was marked in a dull blue: Cargo Bay 4.

Josh glanced straight down at Tate. 'OK, Tate, what's the plan and what the DOOF are we doing in a cargo bay?!'

Tate replied in his ever calm (and, in fact, calming) way, 'Hello Joshua, we must get to the computer core, so I can access the mainframe, and reprogram. Unfortunately, IDF cannot target the source of our troubles directly when they beam us in, they can target the area, or in this case, the ship. I have already scanned the ship, and will display our route to you.'

Josh thought for a moment, and said, 'Well at least they got us *on* the ship!' (Considering to himself that *outside* the ship would not have been good!) 'OK, Tate, let's go.'

Josh immediately broke into a run, towards the large closed steel doorway. Upon arrival, the button was obvious, as it was bigger than Josh's hand.

'Ready, Tate?' said Josh.
'Ready, Josh,' said Tate.

Josh hit the pad, and as the huge door panels slid open shouted, 'Open Sesame!'

'Very amusing, Joshua,' replied Tate, who had not been programmed with a sense of humour.

Josh had already memorised the first part of the route. He strolled out into the much better-lit passageway and took a right turn.

Immediately red lights started to flash all around, and claxons roared. A voice not dissimilar but much sharper than Tate's announced, 'Intruder alert! Intruder alert!'

Josh took in the situation in for a moment, but was soon shocked into action.

'Targeting!' came the next extremely loud announcement. And Josh instantly noticed a series of laser weapons mounted high on the silver walls turning towards him.

The very next moment he was running down the corridor surrounded by a hail of red light as the guns fired. He dove forward and gambolled over one beam as he arrived at the end of the passageway. He had to think quickly now. Left or right? He turned right again, but knew immediately and shouted to himself and Tate, 'It should have been left!'

But there was no stopping now. This corridor had only one door, at the very end. Josh was still running for his life, darting through the laser fire, but he did hear Tate state, 'Hacking access code'.

It was only 50 metres, and Josh arrived there in moments. Just as the light on the panel to the side of the door lit up green and the door slid upwards with a *whooosh*. Josh slid on his knees under the door and as soon as he was through Tate signalled for the door to close behind them.

Then, *blam*! The door was hit by a shot that would have vaporized Josh and Tate.

Josh was still on his knees, looking a bit like a rock

guitarist who had slid across the stage. Somewhat out of breath, he murmured, 'What the doof?'

Tate (of course) as calm as ever, stated, 'It appears that we triggered the intruder alarm system.'

'No kidding, Einstein!' said Josh. Tate was also not programmed to understand sarcasm.

They were now in a much smaller, and somewhat dishevelled room. Unloved, and full of what appeared to be cleaning materials. There was a small console in the corner, with a screen, and a flashing light or two.

Then it occurred to Josh, 'Tate, we're in the broom cupboard!'

'Correct, Joshua. Or perhaps, the cleaning closet?'

'So what the doof are we gonna do now, Tate?!' exclaimed Josh, still reeling from the laser run.

'I believe I may be able to access the ship's computer from that console, Joshua,' said Tate, matter-of-factly.

Josh's eyes lit up as he looked at the dusty old screen in the corner of the broom cupboard.

Chapter 14 Paul

Josh, now regaining his composure after his 'dash for life', walked over to the console. 'OK, Tate, do your stuff.'

'Accessing,' said Tate, matter-of-factly, as always.

Moments later the screen (somewhat cleaner now, as Josh had wiped away the dust with his sleeve) lit up, with the bright red lettering, 'Access Denied – Intruder Alert'.

The klaxons outside the broom cupboard once more wailed, raising Josh's heartbeat a notch or three!

'Tate?' he asked (trying to sound calmer than he really felt).

'One moment, Joshua,' replied Tate. 'Accessing.'

An anxious 30 seconds went by, during which time Josh kept a careful eye on the laser-damaged, but thankfully closed, door panel.

And then the screen lit up once again, this time with just what Josh wanted to see. In bright green lettering, the joy-evoking words, 'Access Granted', accompanied by a satisfying beep. And then the klaxons fell silent.

The screen scrolled to say, 'Ship's Computer. Personal And Universal Logistics, P.A.U.L.'.

'Hmm,' thought Josh, 'Paul.'

The text on the screen then dissolved and the image of a virtual face formed, looking somewhat forlorn, and somewhat comical. Moments later a voice crackled from the speaker next to the screen, and the virtual face spoke to Josh.

'Allo? Who are you?'

Josh knew that time was not on their side. 'Hi Paul, I'm Joshua, I've been sent to help you by the IDF. You are off course and heading into a black hole.'

Josh was a bit taken aback by the response: Paul burst into 'virtual' tears!

'Bwwwaa-hu-hurrr! I don't know what to do! I got attacked, and I've forgotten where to go, and I can't wake the Captain up, and … and … and … Bwuuurrr!'

'Calm down Paul! Josh shouted. 'We're here now and we're going to help you.'

'Th-th-thank you. Bwuurr-hurr-hurr-hurr!' came the bizarre reply.

'Tate, what's the next step?' asked Josh, knowing he needed to be in control, as Paul certainly wasn't.

'I can access Paul's memory systems, Joshua, and reboot him so he can get the ship back on course. We have 30 minutes until the gravitational pull from the black hole becomes too great. But we have another problem. Long-range sensors have detected another IDE ship approaching us with weapons armed. You must get to the main bridge and access weapons control, and fend off their attack.'

'Erm, not too much to do, then!' quipped Josh.

'Time is of the essence, Joshua,' replied Tate. 'I am connected to Paul through wi-fi now. I can guide you to the bridge while I work. Go. Now.'

Josh was moving before Tate finished speaking.

He heard Paul mournfully say 'Bye' behind him as he left the broom closet.

'At least no more tears now,' he murmured to Tate.

Josh sped through the now quiet passageways. The ship was a leviathan, and with a way still to go, he heard Tate announce matter-of-factly, 'Fifteen minutes remaining.'

Josh was now following the route lit up for him by Paul along the corridors, so that Tate could work on repairing the data loss.

'How are you doing, Tate?' asked Josh – not breathlessly (*actual* Josh did not get physically tired).

'I estimate full repair with 32.76 seconds remaining, Joshua.'

Josh's reply of 'Plenty of time then!' was stifled by (once more) the roar of the alert klaxons. And then Paul's voice, 'Bwuurhuurrrrr! (sob). Enemy ship closing! Weapons range in 14 minutes!'

Josh got his head down, and just kept running. Every access door was opened by Tate before he got to it, so he had no need to pause for a moment.

Finally, with relief, Josh entered a much wider corridor and saw a door panel ahead of him which said in impressive lettering, 'Main Bridge'. Even the door was twice as big as anything he had seen. It slid open, corner to corner, almost with grace as Tate accessed it.

And then Josh was there. On the main bridge. A huge impressive area, with many stations and control panels. But what caught Josh's eye was the vision on the view screen: the black hole. Gaping before them, as black as black can be in the middle, but surrounded by a stunning swirl of colour, of light, created by the stars, nebulas and energy drawn into its enormous gravitational well.

But Josh had no time to take this in. As they entered the bridge, Tate announced, 'Three minutes and 30 seconds remaining.' And Paul announced, 'IDE ship has weapons lock.'

Josh knew what he had to do. He sped around the control room, until he spotted the console marked 'Weapons Control'. It was in the centre of the bridge and had its own view screen. Josh jumped straight into the large seat and grabbed the control stick. As he did so he shouted, 'Paul! Arm lasers!'

Paul's upset face appeared on the panel to Josh's left. 'Bwuuuh! Lasers are inoperative Josh!'

At that moment the ship shook as it took a hit from the enemy ship. The black hole momentarily slid out of view as the ship was knocked sideways.

'Damage to cargo bays,' announced Tate. 'Two minutes and 17 seconds remaining.'

'What weapons *have* I got, Paul?' shouted Josh. This was getting close to the wire now.

'BwuuuH! One Tranzluteum torpedo, Joshua. Manual targeting only!' a panicked Paul replied.

Josh knew what he had to do. 'Arm Tranzluteum torpedo, Paul, and engage manual control.'

The bright red word 'Armed' flashed up on the console, and Josh swung round hard to the left on the control stick. His chair span along with his view screen, and then he had the enemy ship in his sights.

Josh had no plans to kill anybody, and also no time to think. The ship was *big*, long and sleek, with a nacelle each side, obviously the engines. Josh set the cross-hairs on the starboard engine. As he fired he saw a green flash of laser fire from the enemy ship.

Moments later the *Aquarius* shook again. They had been hit! And the torpedo turret was destroyed!

'*Bwuuuh!*' said Paul. Again.

But Josh had got his shot away. He watched the trail of the torpedo snake towards the IDE ship, and ... *boooooom!* The starboard engine exploded in a spectacular shower of flames and fireworks.

Josh had nailed it. 'Tate! I did it!' exclaimed Josh.

'Well done, Joshua, I expected nothing less,' replied Tate. 'One minute 47 seconds remaining.'

Josh sat back, just for a moment, hoping that his job was done. 'It's down to Tate now,' he thought. He thought.

'Proximity alert!' was the next thing blurted out by Paul.

'What now?' thought Josh. He looked at his monitor. The heavily damaged IDE ship was now being pulled straight at them by the force of the black hole!

Josh didn't need to be told by Tate what he had to do this time. 'Paul!' he shouted.

'Whuh?! Bluh!' replied Paul, still in a state.

'Can you route fusion drive control to me here?'

'Uhhhh! Bluh! Yes.'

'*Well do it!*'

The panel next to Josh lit up again: 'Fusion Drive – Manual Control'.

Josh had the power of this 50 million ton ship at his fingertips.

He shouted 'Full power!' and jammed the control stick hard to the right. The huge ship started to turn, painfully slowly, as the IDE ship was drawn ever nearer.

As the black hole slid out of view, Josh could see nothing but stars. It looked incredibly peaceful. Just for a moment.

The ship was 270 degrees (three-quarters of the way) round when the IDE battleship, leaving a trail of sparks, passed on its injured way into the black hole. Josh had managed to avoid the collision of two ships a mile long by just 50 metres.

And now they were facing away from the black hole.

At this moment, Tate had something to say. '32.76 seconds remaining. Ship's computer restored, Joshua.'

And suddenly Paul sounded confident and in control. 'Course laid in. Main drive engaged.'

WHHHHHHOOOOOOOOOSSSSSH!

Suddenly the great ship *Aquarius* was travelling at light speed, towards her destination of VEGA XII. In her wake, the IDE battleship slipped powerless into the black hole. Her intended destination for the *Aquarius*.

Josh slumped back into his chair, exhausted. His *actual* body could not tire, but his brain could.

His first thought was for those who had tried to destroy them. 'Tate, what will happen to the people in that ship?'

'We have no definite answers on that, Joshua. All scientific research points to the fact that they will emerge somewhere, on the other side, lost in space.'

'But alive?'

'Yes, alive.'

'Phew,' thought Josh. His job was to save lives, not take them.

And then Paul chipped in, chirpily, 'Emergency situation resolved. Thank you for your help, Tate and Joshua. Procedure dictates that I now awake the Captain.'

'No worries, Paul,' replied Josh. 'Glad to see you have a smile on your face now!' (Paul's virtual face was grinning at him from the control panel.) 'We'll meet you there.'

Josh made his way to the bridge crew's cryogenic sleep chamber, chatting to Tate en route about their amazing adventure. All the corridors were brightly lit now, and Paul smiled at them occasionally as they passed the control screens.

The cryogenic chamber was all in white, in contrast to the many grey corridors they had travelled during the mission.

As Josh walked in, Captain Correlli was climbing out of his cryo bed. Rubbing his eyes and yawning, he looked up at Josh. 'Wh-who are you?' he asked, still in the process of waking.

As the red glow of the IDF transporter began to surround him, Josh said, 'I'm Joshua, from the IDF. Paul will update you.'

'In final approach for Vega XII, Captain,' said Paul.

And as Josh was enveloped in familiar red light,

'Bwuhh! Bye Joshua!' Somehow, a virtual tear ran down his virtual face.

ZZZZZZZZZZZZAP!

And Josh was gone.

And Josh was home.

PART V

THE KID WITH NO NAME (NEMESIS STAGE 1)

Chapter 15 IDF briefing

Location: The Wild West, Planet Earth.
Year: 1873.
Situation: Unclear, the data stream from IDF has been corrupted via an unknown source. *Alarm bells!*
Josh Projection Age: 30.
Mission Objective: Unknown.

Chapter 16 Run for cover

ZZZZZZZZZZAP!
Pyoww!

'What the doof?!' All Josh knew was that he was heading to the Wild West. What he didn't know included the fact that he was to materialise in the middle of a shoot-out!

As the shots rang out Josh was standing in the middle of the high street. Immediately he looked for the nearest bit of cover. He sprinted across the dusty street and gambolled behind a large barrel.

He glanced straight down at his 'watch'. 'Blimey, Tate! Can you give me any info?'

'Our location is Diamond Gulch, in the Mid West, United States of America.'

'Is that it?!'

'Sorry, Joshua, that's all I have for now.'

Josh took in his surroundings. It was a long, sand-coloured street, with a line of wooden buildings either side. He spotted the Sheriff's office (no sign of the Sheriff though), the undertakers – 'I don't plan on going there anytime soon,' mumbled Josh – and right opposite him was the biggest building in the street. It had double swinging doors in the middle and a large sign overhead which simply read 'Saloon'. Several horses were tied loosely by their reins outside. Josh was amazed they weren't spooked by the gunfire. Maybe they were used to it.

Talking of gunfire, it had stopped! Moments later a lone cowboy sprinted past, down the street, and out of town on his horse. A voice chased him, shouting 'And don't come back! Stay away from my woman, ya varmint!'

'It seems we have been privy to a domestic dispute, Joshua,' stated Tate, as Josh stood up and dusted himself off. (Man, it was dusty!)

'Wow, Tate,' Josh replied. 'What an introduction to the Wild West! Have you been able to contact IDF about our mission?'

'All we know, Joshua, is that we are in the right place, at the right time.'

'OK, then, let's go looking for trouble!'

Josh didn't mean that literally, he simply knew that they were there for a reason. More than likely to *stop* some trouble.

He could now relax for a moment, and look around. He glanced down at his own outfit. He was wearing the full complement of the attire of a gunslinger: long coat, leather chaps, boots, spurs, and a pair of Colt .44 pistols in low-slung holsters clipped to his belt and strapped onto each leg. He reached up and touched the brim of his – yes – Stetson hat.

As he scratched an itch on his chin he noticed … stubble! 'Hmm, that's a new one,' thought Josh.

The street was now abuzz with people going about their business. A young lady selling flowers, a horse-drawn carriage trundling by, people gathering in groups talking and laughing. Just like nothing had happened only five minutes ago!

A tumbleweed rolled past right in front of Josh. He sniggered. 'Just like the movies.'

He made his mind up to head straight into the saloon. Probably the best place to get the feel of what was going on in Diamond Gulch.

The sun blazed down from a clear blue sky as Josh strolled across the street, with his spurs making that familiar clinking noise. He felt equally nervous and excited. He knew that there was serious work to do, but heck, how many times had he played 'cowboy' as a youngster? He decided not to actually try and do a cowboy walk. He opted for simply, the 'Josh walk'.

There was music and sounds of frivolity coming from inside the bar. He arrived at the swinging doors, took a deep breath, and went in.

He was certain that silence would fall and all eyes would be upon him, but, no, it was not like in the movies (thankfully!): Everyone totally ignored him and carried on with, well, whatever they were doing. There was a couple of tables surrounded by mean-looking guys playing cards, some people just drinking, and a violin, banjo and washboard trio stomping out some tunes in the corner. Along with several drunken fellows, and some very pretty ladies dancing nearby.

Josh made his way to the bar, where a very beautiful young lady, with her white-blonde hair pinned up into a spectacular Old West style danced over to him.

'Well hi there, stranger! What're y'all doin' in these parts?' she asked with a glorious grin.

Josh hesitated for a moment, he was used to talking to girls of his age at school, but this was a different league!

'Erm ... well, I'm not quite sure yet, ma'am.' He replied, automatically putting on his best Western accent (as learned from Marty McFly in *Back to The Future 3*).

'You sure do look confused, handsome! I tell you what, let me get you some suppin' whisky. My name's Babs, and this is my saloon. Y'all are welcome here, as long as you don't pull out them shootin' irons!'

As she went to get Josh his drink, he raised his wrist to his arm and whispered to Tate, 'Shootin' irons?'

Josh felt a vibration on his wrist. Tate had gone into

stealth mode so as not to arouse wonderment from the locals. In fact, to the locals he didn't look like a watch from the future, he was seen as only a gathering of worn leather bracelets.

Josh looked at the screen. 'Shootin' irons = guns'. And then moments later: 'Suppin' whisky is a strong alcoholic beverage. Alcohol has no effect on you during mission placement thankfully, Joshua. And of course you are far too young for such things. However you will taste it.'

'OK, Dad!' Josh quietly and sarcastically replied just as Babs plonked a (not very clean-looking) glass and a bottle in front of him.

'There y'are young man, that'll be 2 cents a slug.'

Josh had no idea if IDF had furnished him with funds! He tapped several pockets before he heard a chink. He grabbed a handful and dropped about eight small gold coins on the bar.

'Why thank you!' said Babs joyfully. 'I think I'll leave that bottle right here.' She reached over the bar, wrapped her arms around Josh's neck, pulled him towards her and planted a big smacker on his cheek!

Josh then found out that he COULD blush whilst on an IDF transmission. But he had to focus on the job in hand.

'Have a drink with me, Babs,' he said as he picked up the dusty bottle. (So much dust!)

'Well, I don't mind if I do! You've made my day, handsome stranger!'

Babs plonked another glass down, and as he filled them, Babs took on a more serious demeanour. 'I think I do know why you're here. It's because of the bandit ain't it.' It wasn't even a question. It was a statement.

Josh looked straight into her glistening blue eyes, but as he was about to enquire about this bandit she boisterously shouted 'Cheers!', clinked her glass into his and drank it down in one.

'Uh-oh!' Thought Josh, 'got to do it!' So he followed suit and swallowed the lot.

A moment later: Urgh! Argh! Bleurch!! Josh attempted to the max to hide his fervent disgust at what he had just tasted. He tried to stop water streaming from his *actual reality* eyes, as he made his best attempt at maintaining Babs's initial impression of him as 'the handsome stranger'.

Babs continued, 'They say he's called Kasabian. He's been blazing a trail through the Mid West. Robbin' banks, stage coaches, payrolls, any darn thing he comes across. There's five thousand bucks on his head. Thing is, no one ever knows where he'll strike next.'

Josh listened to what she said, recovering from his first (and probably last!) taste of 'supping whisky'. As he put his glass down on the bar, he felt a now familiar buzz on his wrist. And he knew: this was the mission.

Chapter 17 The runaway train (goes down the track)

As if on cue, Josh suddenly heard screams outside the saloon. Followed by a gunshot. One of the dancing girls bravely ran to the window, 'It's the Bandit!' she shouted.

Rather than running outside, guns blazing, most of the men in the bar seemed to be jumping under the tables. Kasabian was feared.

Josh looked back at Babs. 'Yes, that's why I'm here,' he said. He leaned over, and cheekily kissed her on the cheek, said 'Take care, darlin',' and sprinted for the door.

As the swing doors creakily waved goodbye, Josh was back in the sunshine. A lone rider stormed down the street, dressed all in black. 'Yeeeeeeeehaw!' he yelled, as he galloped by, shooting into the sky.

Josh didn't hesitate, he was down the steps in a blink, and mounting one of the horses outside the saloon. 'Ya!' he shouted as he began his pursuit.

He was about 500 yards behind the bandit as they sped out of town. Clouds of dust rose from the hooves of the bandit's horse. Immediately Josh noticed that the bandit was riding parallel to the train tracks, and there was a train coming through!

Josh utilised the few horse-riding lessons he'd had as a youngster to encourage his steed to go as fast as *actually* possible. 'What the doof, Tate!' he shouted. 'I've never ridden this fast before!'

As Kasabian drew alongside the train, Josh was now

only 200 yards behind. He watched closely as the villain stepped almost gracefully from his horse onto the back of the rear carriage, and disappeared inside with his bag of loot.

Josh was there moments later. But his boarding of the train was far less ceremonious. He slightly misjudged his moment to leap, as his horse swerved dangerously to avoid a ditch. Josh found himself clinging to the rear railings of the carriage, as his sturdy boots dragged behind.

Somehow he dragged himself aboard. He didn't have time to enjoy the fact that he was onboard a proper steam train back in the day, nor to gaze at the scenery, nor to listen to the powerful choof-ing noise from the engine.

As he dusted himself off, concealed behind the wooden door of the carriage, he spoke to Tate. 'Location of Kasabian, Tate?' he said firmly. No time for joking around right now.

'Three carriages ahead, Joshua. And no further movement. I believe he thinks he has not been followed.'

'Right,' said Josh. He planned to act as 'just another passenger'. He slowly opened the door, and began to make his way carefully, and nonchalantly through the first carriage. It was tightly packed, and very smoky. Full of 'Western folk', just as Josh would have imagined them. The seats encaptured tables, in the fashion of the booths you might see in a bar (a more modern bar!). And all were socialising. Some had 'suppin' whisky'. 'Bleh!' thought Josh.

Some of the men glanced warily at Josh, as he supposed they would, seeing a gunslinger strolling by. But Josh made it through without incident.

The second carriage was much the same.

There was a somewhat louder party of three cowboys and three dames at the far end of the carriage. Just as Josh approached the door a particularly mean-looking fella stood up in his way and turned to face him. Josh looked him straight in the ... chest! This guy must have been 6 foot 7. He had to duck to stand up!

As Josh braced himself, the tall guy said, 'Hic! 'Scuse me, stranger.' And politely made his way past. Phew!

Josh continued through. Moments later he was at the door to the third carriage. Tate suddenly beeped, and said, 'Suspect is on the move, Joshua!'

Without hesitation Josh opened the door. His right hand reaching for his holstered Colt .44.

Kasabian was standing at the far end of the carriage, with the (right-hand) side door open. He looked Josh straight in the eye and said, 'Too late again, Joshua.'

All Josh could think was, 'How does he know my name?'

And as he thought that, Kasabian leapt from the train. The snigger of 'Hahaa!' trailed behind him.

Chapter 18 Endgame

As the folks in this carriage watched in wonder, Josh sprinted down the aisle, and without hesitating jumped out after Kasabian.

When he finally stopped rolling in the dust (yes, more dust), Josh noticed that they had disembarked on the leading edge of the next town along the line from Diamond Gulch. Kasabian, of course, had jumped 200 yards before Josh, and was only now running into town. Josh was up in moments. Up and running. He had both guns drawn. But he wouldn't shoot to kill. Josh would *never* shoot to kill.

'Stop, Kasabian! You can't get away!' shouted Josh. And he actually fired a shot from each pistol into the air as a warning. A hundred yards ahead, Josh only heard Kasabian laugh out loud again.

Kasabian was running straight up the centre of 'Main Street', as Josh assumed it would be called. And Josh decided to race behind the first section of wooden buildings on the left in an attempt to cut him off. He sprinted past six or seven places before cutting through a gully onto the street.

And there was Kasabian. Slap bang in the middle of the street. Holding a very pretty and scared-looking young lady. 'Now, this is how it's gonna go, Joshua,' said Kasabian, with a glint in his eye and a glint on his until now unnoticed gold tooth. 'Me and this here pretty darlin' are gonna ride out of town. And you ain't gonna follow. That way she gets to see her momma and her pappa tomorrow. Understand?'

At that moment the sun was high in the sky, and it was baking hot. But all the people in the town were frozen still.

'Disarm, Joshua,' said Tate.

Josh stared straight back into the dark eyes of Kasabian. That moment seemed to last an age. And then Josh slowly and carefully reholstered his weapons.

'Heheh' was the gloating sound that emerged from Kasabian's lips. Kasabian glanced around the street. He raised his gun nonchalantly to aim at a crowd near the saloon. 'You sir, bring that there horse over for me.'

'M-m-m-m-me?' stuttered the somewhat portly middle-aged man in the centre.

'Well, hell. You'll do!' replied Kasabian, followed by a somewhat maniacal cackle. Something along the lines of 'Ki-hi-hi-hi!'

The frightened fellow unhitched the first horse in the line and walked it over to Kasabian. Kasabian mounted the horse, and gun still trained on him, said, 'Now, y'all help this pretty little thing aboard.'

The moment she was, Kasabian shouted, 'Now dance!' and began shooting around his feet. To the backing track of 'Ki-hi-hi-hi!' and '*Pyow! Bang! Pwoom!*' the frightened fellow jumped, dived, and survived.

And now Kasabian was galloping down the street with his loot, and his hostage.

Another rough-looking man, and young for a cowboy (maybe 18?) had snuck up next to Josh. He whispered to Josh, 'Hey man, I like your style. My name's Billy. Try my new Winchester.' And handed Josh a rifle.

'I recommend caution,' said Tate, matter-of-factly as always.

Josh took aim as Kasabian sped north, approaching the edge of town. Josh knew exactly what he was aiming for. Moments passed and no one breathed. The only sound was that of the horse's speeding hooves.

Josh fired. And hit! the chain on the sign that said, 'Now leaving Diamond Creek'. And as Kasabian sped past, the sign swung down, and knocked him clean off the horse!

Everyone in the town was running. Josh and Billy got there first. The young lady jumped off the horse and ran to embrace Josh. 'Why thank you, sir, thank you so much!' she screamed so, so joyously.

But Josh was only interested in Kasabian right now, and stood over him.

Kasabian gazed, dazed, up at Josh. And said, 'I'll be back for you Joshua. Ki-hi-hi-hi!'

BLLLLLLLLLLLAP!

And Kasabian was gone.

And Kasabian was home.

'What the doof?!' exclaimed Josh.

'Well I'll be,' said Billy. 'And what's your name, sir? I'm thinking we could work together some time.'

'I don't know about that,' said Josh, as the red glowing beams began to surround him.

ZZZZZZZZZZZZAP!

And Josh was gone.

And Josh was home.

Josh's first thought once home was, 'I've gotta talk to Dad.'

Chapter 19 IDF log, supplemental

Before Josh could sleep that night, he emailed his dad. He had to know: what was going on? Who was Kasabian? How did he know who Josh was? Questions that wouldn't help him sleep too well. But of course, he knew the mission had been a success, so when he did dream it was of riding fast and saving pretty young ladies. (Luckily no dreams of 'supping whisky'!)

The reply read thus:

> To: Kidda
> From: Daddio
>
> Hey Kidda, I was hoping you wouldn't have to face a mission such as this yet. Unfortunately there are some bad guys out there. I guess, without the bad guys, us good guys wouldn't have a job, huh? ;-)
> Well, you've had your first encounter with the IDE. That's the Inter Dimensional Empire. Out there, in the bigger scheme of things, they want to rule, whilst we work only — I know it's a cliché — 'to serve and protect'.
> I have had many encounters with a guy from the IDE, name of Dan Raven. I still do. And Kasabian is his son. I believe this was his first mission. And you *got* him.
> 1-0 to the good guys, Kidda. In this case they were actually trying to rearrange Earth's history. And that guy Billy you met? Billy The Kid. He wasn't a good guy either.

But our job is to protect our history. And our future. We can't change the past.

I'm sure you will see Kasabian again. I hope not for a while.

Keep it up, Kidda. Commendation!

Lotsa Love,
Daddio.

Josh sat back in his chair with just one thought, 'Wow!'

PART VI
DESERT ISLAND JOSH

Chapter 20 IDF briefing

Location: Planet Earth, 2016, a small island in the Pacific Ocean.
Situation: A young girl, the same age as Josh (the same real age) has found herself alone on a desert island.
Josh Projection Age: 12
Mission Objective: Get her rescued!

Chapter 21 Survive the storm

ZZZZZZZZAP!

From the mission brief, Josh knew to be prepared, but, 'What the doof?' Josh crouched immediately to avoid the wind blowing him over as it thrashed the trees on the shore, and lashed the rain into his eyes.

He looked around for a moment, taking in his surroundings. It was night time, and he was on a beach. Huge waves bristled with froth as they were thrown onto the shoreline by the raging wind. The moon occasionally very briefly appeared between the ferocious-looking clouds, which gave Josh just enough light. A long line of palm trees further up the beach seemed almost to dance in the wind.

'Tate!' he shouted above the bluster, 'do we have a location on the young lady in need?'

Josh held Tate up to his ear, and heard the calm reply. 'Yes, Joshua, she is 63.76 metres directly ahead.'

'What the doof?!' Josh could see nothing ahead but flailing trees and rocks. Quite a few big rocks.

'Behind the largest boulder, Joshua,' said Tate.

'Ah. Boulders. Yes, boulders.'

Josh sprang forward, and as he got to 20 metres away he heard her for the first time. A scream so powerful that it made it to his ears even against the wind. As he sped towards her he tripped on what looked like a huge plank of driftwood. He scrambled back to his feet, and then he was only feet away. He could see her clinging to the edge of a boulder by her fingertips, her whole body lifted into the air by the gale that assaulted them.

Just as she lost her grip, Josh dived forward and wrapped his arms around her. They both fell into the relative shelter behind the rock.

They lay there for a moment, and then the young girl looked up at Josh. 'Th-th-thank you,' she said tearfully. 'Wh-who are you?'

'I'm Josh,' he replied calmly, 'and I'm here to help. What's your name?'

'I'm S-S-S-Cindy,' she stuttered, holding Josh very tightly. She didn't want to let go.

'OK, Cindy. What we have to do right now is ride out this storm. I know you're scared, I am too. You stay right here for now.'

'B-B-B-But!'

'Don't worry, I know what I'm doing.'

Josh had one thing on his mind: shelter. And perhaps it had actually been a huge stroke of luck that he tripped on that large plank of driftwood moments earlier. He freed himself from Cindy's grip, and made his way back to it. It was about 6 feet long, and 5 feet wide. 'Perfect,' thought Josh.

He reached down and heaved the shoreward end to hip height. All the time the wind blasting him with sand from the beach. He turned and began to drag it back towards Cindy, the blow at his back now. He only hoped that it wouldn't launch the driftwood into the air from behind him. He was literally thinking on his feet. Tate could do nothing to help him right now. Josh knew what he wanted to do, he knew what he *had* to do.

He struggled and worked, and dragged the plank past Cindy, to another huge boulder about 30 feet further, just before the tree line. This one was about 4 feet high (about 30 feet wide, but that didn't matter), and not too craggy on top, fairly level. Josh heaved one end of the plank to the top of it (about head height for *actual* 12-year-old Josh). And then he set about finding smaller rocks to anchor the makeshift roof into the sand.

Some of them were almost too heavy to carry, but he knew they needed to be.

Once he was happy they would hold, he went back for Cindy, took her hand very tightly, and they got under the shelter.

Thankfully there was some foliage just in front of the rock, which made their position slightly more bearable. And with the huge gale blowing directly onshore, they were well sheltered from both the wind, and the rain.

Josh was more than happy to let Cindy once more hold him tightly, he felt like he needed a hug, to be honest! She let out a very sorrowful whimper, and Josh just said, 'All we can do is try to rest now, Cindy. And hope that it will have blown over come morning.'

Josh didn't feel like resting, the adrenaline was still surging through his *actual* body. But he knew he must: this adventure had only just begun.

Then there was a calming beep from his wrist. 'Well done, Joshua. Dawn is in 6 hours 18 minutes. Weather forecast: Fine.'

'Hmm?' said Cindy, already almost asleep. She must have been shattered.

'That's my friend Tate,' said Josh. 'I'll introduce you in the morning.'

And relieved that the storm would indeed pass, Josh soon slept too.

Chapter 22 The coconut incident

Josh awoke to a very subtle beep from Tate. Cindy was still fast asleep in his arms. The shelter had held firm, and just outside the edges of the roof, Josh could see clear blue sky! There was barely a breeze, and he even heard the sounds of seagulls looking for their breakfast.

Josh carefully slid out from under Cindy, not wanting to wake her, and stepped outside. Beautiful crisp morning air, the sun blazing across (not down on, as it had only just risen above the horizon) the very beautiful blue Pacific Ocean.

'OK,' thought Josh, 'breakfast for Cindy, and then a plan.' He strolled down the beach, and looked at Tate. Tate was actually looking a bit worse for wear, covered in sand, and with a crown of a small piece of seaweed!

'Morning, Tate!' said Josh, now actually buzzing, as the mission thus far had been a success. 'So, er, what's the plan?' was his following question. His euphoria immediately somewhat tainted by the realisation that he had no clue what to do next.

'Good morning, Joshua,' said Tate, as Josh dusted him off and removed his green headdress. 'The search for Cindy is taking place. However they have not taken this vicinity into consideration as, apparently, they do not believe she could have travelled this far and survived.'

'Erm ... OK. What do I have to do, Tate?'

'According to IDF forecasts, the search pattern will progress to 5 miles north of here by approximately midnight tonight, Joshua.'

'Erm,' (again) 'north?' Josh looked out to sea. Josh knew from where the sun was rising that north was straight out there, thataway, to sea.

'Yes Joshua, north.'

Josh had only one thought in his head. 'Raft, Tate?'

'Raft, Joshua.'

Josh knew what the plan was now, and he also knew that 5 miles was a long way to go, on a raft. So time was of the essence.

He was about to begin his search for breakfast when he noticed a large wooden chest on the beach. It was a long way up the beach from where the waves were now quietly washing in, but not far from Josh. He made straight for it. It was old, the kind of thing that people would make long voyages with many moons ago. But it was in bizarrely good condition. And upon closer examination he found an engraved name plate on it. 'George Roper'. And underneath, 'Miss Cindy Roper'.

'What the doof?!' said Josh out loud. 'OK, this can't be a coincidence.' So he immediately took it by the sturdy leather handle on one end, and began to drag it up the beach towards the shelter. 'Doing a lot of dragging things, this mission,' moaned Josh as he made his way back to Cindy.

As he got back to base there was a delighted yelp from Cindy. 'You found it!' she (almost) shouted as she galloped over.

'Good morning to you too, Cindy,' said Josh. 'Have you got some fresh clothes in there?' Cindy was looking somewhat bedraggled.

'Yes!' Cindy hurriedly undid the heavy leather straps on the chest, grabbed some garments which were right on top and disappeared back into their shelter. Two minutes later she bounced out in bright blue dungarees

('Dungarees?' thought Josh), a spanking clean white T-shirt, and she had even brushed her red hair and tied it back into a pony tail.

'OoooooooK,' said Josh. 'Now. I've gotta get you some breakfast.'

'That's OK! I've got that too!' said Cindy. She was full of the joy of life, having survived the previous night.

Cindy lifted the top compartment in the chest, underneath were several more compartments. She opened the one on the right, which contained a plethora of culinary delights. (In a snack kinda way!) Sandwiches, crisps, pork pies, cakes, fruit, etcetera etcetera etcetera.

'What would you like, Josh?' she asked, her eyes smiling up at him.

'I'm OK, Cindy, I want *you* to eat, you need to get your strength back.' (Josh, of course, didn't need to *actually* eat, and he wanted Cindy to keep all her provisions.)

As Cindy sat down in the sunshine with her breakfast, Josh had to ask: 'OK, Cindy, I need you to tell me how you ended up here.'

Cindy teared up again a little bit, as she told Josh of her harrowing tale. She had been travelling with her father, on one of the world's last running steam ships, en route to Hawaii. Her cabin was only three away from her dad's, and one night (two nights ago), she couldn't sleep through excitement, and decided to drag her dad's beloved travel chest from her cabin to her dad's, to surprise him in the morning. (He had piles of other luggage, but she knew how he loved his antique chest.) Little did she know, that he wanted it in her cabin, as he knew that she loved it too.

That night, the storm was only starting, and as she struggled to pull the chest, she wrapped both her arms around the straps on the top. She had got past two cabins when the ship had lurched to the port (left) and both she and the chest slid towards the side. Five seconds later, another lurch, and *sploooosh*! They had both gone over the side.

Thankfully the sturdy container was very buoyant, and they resurfaced in a moment. However, as the steam ship slowly moved away, of course, no one could hear Cindy's cries for help. And no one would even know she was missing until the morning.

She had clung to her now 'liferaft' overnight, and throughout the next day, before somehow escaping injury when virtually surfing onto the beach, where Josh had saved her.

'And then I ran up the beach, and ... and I held on, and ... and then you were there, Josh.'

Josh put his arm around her again, as she finished off a cheese and onion sandwich, two apples, and an orange.

'OK!' said Josh. 'I'm gonna get you back to your dad. First things first. You need a drink. Have you got water in your magic chest?' he said with a wink.

'No,' replied Cindy, 'I kept all my cola under my bunk!'

'Hmm,' thought Josh out loud. He looked at the trees just behind their little house. 'I know!'

As Josh made his way to the trees, he started to scan the ground.

Cindy stared after him in wonder. 'What are you looking for, Josh?'

Josh had spotted them all around, plucked from the trees by the now faded wind.

He turned round, looked at Cindy and spread his arms wide. Just as he said the word 'Coconuts!' there was also a *bonk*, as one of them that had survived the gale picked that moment to fall, and bounced off Josh's head.

Cindy fell on the floor laughing! And as Josh began to blush, he thought he actually heard a little electronic snigger come from his wristwatch. 'Shaddap, Tate!' said Josh, as he too began to laugh. And moments later the rapturous laughter surrounded them.

Once they had recovered from their impromptu hilarity, Josh gathered a large pile of coconuts. He utilised a sharp stone to crack several of them open so that Cindy could have some much-needed rehydration. He kept the one that had bonked him on the head, scratched a smiley face on it, and called it 'Dave'.

But now it was time to get back to the mission.

Chapter 23 How to build a boat, by Joshua Mantra

Josh had formulated a plan for their seaward adventure. Not one raft, but two. The second would be towed behind, and was there only to act as a distress flare.

He asked Cindy to scour the beach in search of anything that may be of use which had washed up ashore. Mainly rope, and anything that would float!

As midday approached, Cindy had accumulated quite a pile of (possibly) useful stuff. Josh had positioned the plank, (formerly their roof) at the high tide mark. It would now make the perfect deck for their raft. He then carefully selected some fallen branches from trees further inland, eight to be exact, and positioned them, four a side under the deck of their beloved plank, which was now very much starting to look like a sea-going vessel. Josh had many lengths of vine, which he had cut from the undergrowth ashore. With a huge rusty nail that Cindy had found, and a large rock, he punctured holes in their trusty plank, through which he could pull the vines, to secure the branches.

Small bits of old worn rope that Cindy had discovered were used for extra strength on the 'bow' and 'stern' of their craft.

Cindy had also found a very old and ragged piece of tarpaulin, which Josh knew immediately could be utilised as a sail of sorts.

By 2 pm Josh had made more use of the many pieces

of flotsam and jetsam found by Cindy, pulling smaller rusty nails out of old wood, and hammering them back into more old wood. The successful result being – a mast! On which they could raise their tarpaulin sail.

The day, weather wise, was turning out to be stunning. The calm *after* the storm as it were. And they sat down in the shade for a moment whilst Cindy ate some lunch. As it turned out, a ham and pickle sandwich and a pork pie this time. (Followed of course, by a coconut.)

'How come you haven't eaten, Josh?' asked Cindy, looking bewildered. 'Well, that's kinda hard to explain,' Josh replied. And as he struggled to find the words to say to her, he was rescued by a calming beep from his wrist.

'High tide and optimum launch time is at 6.18 pm, Joshua. The wind is blowing southerly (to the north), so you will be able to utilise the sail.'

Cindy was now sitting with her mouth wide open, halfway through a bite of her sandwich. She managed to close her mouth and, 'Mmmf ... wha ...? What's that?!'

'I told you I was going to introduce you, Cindy. This is Tate!' Josh thought carefully about his next words. 'You know how you have your phone, and it has apps and all that? Well, Tate is the very latest version, and he's a watch.'

'Blimey!' exclaimed Cindy.

'Well said, Joshua,' said Tate. 'You may as well compare me to a sundial. Or perhaps an abacus.'

It seemed that Tate had taken the hump from his description for a moment, but of course, Josh couldn't tell Cindy that he was in fact a projected sentient computer from the Inter-Dimensional Federation, really now, could he?!

'Pleased to meet you, Cindy,' was Tate's final word on the matter.

Next, Cindy sounded like Josh for a moment, when all she could say was, 'Woooowwww!'

After lunch they got straight back to work. Josh on the second 'distress flare' raft, whilst Cindy tightly attached the multitude of buoyant containers she had found to raft number one. From milk containers, to soda bottles, even old 1 gallon plastic petrol cans. She lashed them with vines, between the lines of branches already in place under 'Mr Plank' as they now called 'him'. 'Everything helps,' Josh had told her. 'Just make sure it is *very* tight, so it can't move.'

Josh used a similar system for raft two, which was much smaller, though. And it was alongside at the high water mark on the beach. The deck was a much smaller piece of planking. He had no idea what it had served as before, but it was very dry, and very old. 'This will be nicely flammable,' Josh murmured to Tate.

Two branches were used each side underneath this time, and the raft was piled high with driftwood and sticks.

Josh saved Cindy's best finds until last: a 50 foot piece of bedraggled rope, with which he attached the two rafts together, so that they could tow raft number two. And an old wooden oar, which he could use to paddle out, and then as a rudder.

And they were ready.

Chapter 24 First star on the right, and straight on till morning

It was 6.15 pm. Joshua was looking at the craft he had built, and he felt quite proud, although he knew they hadn't been tested yet! And he hoped his dad would be proud too.

'I want to name our boat, Josh!' Cindy said excitedly. 'Can you think of one?'

'Well,' Josh replied, 'let's call her *Cohuna.*'

'What's that?' Cindy looked at him quizzically.

'It's the name of my dad's yacht back home. And she's never let us down.'

At 6.18, as surely as the sun sets, there was a beep from Tate. And the high tide had the water lapping around both *Cohuna*, and raft number two. (Sadly, raft number two had not been christened!)

They had already lifted the chest onto the stern of their sturdy craft, and now it was time to get her afloat. She weighed a *lot*!

Josh asked Cindy to help him pull her forward. They wrapped their hands in the carefully prepared vine and rope loops (again tied through trusty 'Mr Plank'), and then… 'HEAVE!' shouted Josh. There was little movement at first. But then, inch by inch, Cohuna started to move forwards. 'Heave!', and moments later, she was floating in the shallow surf.

By this time, raft number two had already floated of her own accord. So as Cindy climbed aboard the good ship

Cohuna, Josh pulled her (*Cohuna*) out as far as he could. At shoulder depth in the water he scrambled aboard, grabbed the oar, and began to paddle. He was sitting right in the bow (at the front), and he had the oar between his knees, paddling with all his *actual* might.

As they made their way through the surf, some of the waves seemed to push them backwards. And as the water sprayed, Josh heard the occasional frightened cry from Cindy. But he had to focus. The weight of the chest, and Cindy at the stern (the back) kept the raft balanced. And after 15 minutes (that felt like a lifetime!) they were clear. And so was raft number two.

Josh paddled on for another ten minutes, to make sure they wouldn't fall back into the surf, and then he felt content that they were safe. For now. He made his way astern past the mast to Cindy, to make sure she was OK.

'I'm fine now, Josh. You did *so* well! I can't wait to see my dad!'

'You know what, Cindy? Same here,' replied Josh with a twinkle in his eye. 'OK, time to raise the mainsail!'

Josh was very thankful for the bits of rope Cindy had found on the beach as they hoisted the old tarpaulin.

'One man's junk is another man's treasure, Joshua,' beeped Tate.

Josh tied the old wooden oar in at the stern of *Cohuna*, between two short hollow pieces of bamboo he had carefully positioned earlier. And then, with Josh at the helm, they were sailing.

Two hours slipped serenely by as the breeze pushed them towards their intended destination. Josh had moved Cindy's chest amidships so that their raft wasn't too heavy at the back.

Josh heard a very welcome beep from Tate. 'With the tide pushing us outwards and the wind in our sail we are making a very impressive 2.3 knots, Joshua. That puts us well on course to be discovered by the search party.'

'Sweet, Tate,' replied Josh. 'That's just the news I wanted to hear.'

He glanced around at the now dusky horizon. The island they had left was a tiny dot behind them. Josh took in a deep breath of the salty air he had grown to love through sailing with his dad, and relaxed for a moment. And then ...

Scratch! 'In days of old when ships were bold, just like the men who sailed them!'

'What the doof?!'

'And if they showed us disrespect we'd tie them up and flail them!'

'Huh?!'

'Hoist the Jolly Roger! Hoist the Jolly Roger!'

Music was coming from the chest! And Cindy was singing along. Unbeknownst to Josh, another layer down in the magic chest, was Cindy's dad's incredibly retro, and yet modern (as it ran on batteries) record player!

'It's my dad's favourite band, Josh! And I thought this song was perfect!' shouted Cindy over the music.

'I can't believe it!' replied Josh, 'it's my dad's fave band too! Adam and The Ants!'

As dusk became night, Josh and Cindy enjoyed a multitude of music from her dad's vinyl record collection within the chest. The records didn't even jump as *Cohuna* was pushed on gently by both the waves and the breeze. Until eventually at around 11 pm the batteries died. The last thing they heard was a haunting downward sloping 'Her name is Rioooooooooooo' from another 1980s band called Duran Duran.

Thankfully the silence wasn't too daunting. The moon was full, and they could see quite a way away, with the moonlight and starlight bouncing off the gentle waves.

But less uplifting news was about to come from Tate. 'Joshua, the wind has dropped and we are now only making 0.8 knots. We must make 1.5 in order to be seen by the search party.'

'Suggestions, Tate? I'm guessing you're going to say "paddle"?'

'Yes, Joshua. I recommend that you paddle, *immediately.*'

Josh quickly removed the old oar from its placement at the stern. And from being a rudder, it became a paddle again.

Josh resumed his position at the bow, and paddled, once more with all his might. Cindy sat atop the chest, amidships. Knowing that her very future depended on his efforts, Josh did all he could. He kept on going, ploughing forward. *Cohuna* had lived up to all hopes and expectations, and raft number two followed silently.

'1.7 knots,' said Tate at one moment, and then, '1.1 knots,' a moment later.

Come midnight, they were still half a mile shy of being spotted in the southern section of the search area. Josh spotted the light of a helicopter in the sky in the distance, and Cindy yelled out at the faint sound of the rotor blades.

'Now is the time, Joshua,' said Tate, in a calm voice that surpassed the calm of the quiet sea that surrounded them.

'OK,' replied Josh as he laid down the ever-faithful oar.

As he rushed to the back of the boat, he removed Tate from his arm. He pressed a small button on the right-hand side of Tate and said quietly, so as not to alarm Cindy, 'Set self-destruct. Ten seconds.'

Tate replied with a beep. 'Self-destruct set. See you on the next mission, Joshua.'

It took Josh a brief moment to spot raft number 2. She had floated a little closer and to the port side in the last few seconds. He took aim and threw Tate high through the air towards the raft, Tate beeping the seconds by.

And then Tate landed. Slap bang in the middle of the pile of branches and driftwood. Then: beep. *Bang! Whoooosh!* Raft number two became a blazing beacon in the night.

Josh sped back to Cindy's side and held her for one last time. 'It's OK, Cindy. They're gonna find us now.'

Sure enough, within a minute the helicopter was close by, with a light shining directly onto them. The rotor noise was loud, and the downward sweep of wind was throwing the sea up around them. With three clicks Josh released the tarpaulin sail so it could blow away harmlessly.

'We have you. Stay calm,' came a voice via a megaphone from above.

Cindy looked up at Josh. 'I don't know how to thank you, Josh,' she said.

'Just think of me whenever you hoist the Jolly Roger,' Josh smiled back with a wink.

ZZZZZZZZZZAP!

And Josh was gone.

And Josh was home.

PART VII
IDF TRAINING

Chapter 25 IDF briefing

Location: IDF Headquarters, the Starship *Astron*, Delta Sector.
Year: Now.
Situation: Josh has been called to Headquarters for training. He has no idea what this entails!
Josh Projection Age: 12.
Mission Objective: Unknown.

Chapter 26 The IDF *Astron* (IDF Headquarters)

ZZZZZZZZZZAP!

Josh had been here previously, just before he started his first mission against that huge dinosaur. He had a few moments to have a good look around this time, and he gazed at the huge view screen at the front, which in turn gazed out at the stars.

There was a gold plate mounted proudly on the wall near the view screen, which stated: 'IDF *Astron*. Alpha class exploration and battle ship'. And underneath: 'Captain and Commander: Cat Mantra'.

'Wow,' thought Josh. And just as he did, the gleaming white bridge doors swept open.

'Allo, Kidda!' exclaimed his dad as he walked in, dressed in an equally glowing white and very smart uniform. (At this point Josh realised that he was wearing the same uniform!)

'Hiya Dad!' Josh couldn't contain his excitement at seeing his dad in the *actual* flesh, and ran over for an immediate hug.

'Let's sit down and have a chat, Kidda,' said Cat, and led Josh back round to the front of the bridge. Cat sat down in the central and imperious Captain's chair and beckoned Josh to take a seat next to him. He explained how, although he and Josh were projected onto the *Astron*, the ship was very much *really* there, and constructed of titanium. And how on board the ship, Dad and the crew patrolled and protected the people of the Galaxy. Concluding with, 'This is my main job now, Kidda. You're the one with the away missions!'

Cat-Dad commended Josh on his success thus far. 'Coupla close ones there, Kidda, but I'm really chuffed, and very proud of you.'

'Cheers, Dad!' replied Josh. 'Actually, I think they were *all* close ones!'

'Haha!' Josh's dad laughed, with pride in his eyes. 'We've decided to give you your next step in reaction and targeting training. We want to keep you sharp.'

'Any clue on what it is, Daddio?' replied Josh.

'Sorry, Kidda, no clues! It wouldn't be a true test of your reactions if you knew what was coming!' smiled Dad Mantra. 'Three different scenarios. Ready?'

'Ready as I'll ever be, Dad!'

'OK, Kidda, let's do it.'

And the warm red tendrils of light began to encapsulate Josh.

Chapter 27 Daddio invaders

ZZZZZZZZZZAP!

Josh was sitting in the control station of what appeared to be a ship, facing vertically (that is, straight up, as if in the cockpit of an Apollo spacecraft before launch). He had a control joystick in each hand, each with a trigger button. He looked upwards (straight ahead to him), and could see a huge armada of silver space craft above him. Crabbing sideways through the sky, they had large mechanical claws opening and closing as they moved. And he heard a gradually lowering musical tone (something along the lines of 'Dum-dum-dum-dum').

As one of them opened its claws directly above him, it fired a huge laser bolt at him! Josh swiftly pushed the joystick in his left hand to the right, and avoided getting hit. He found himself behind a defensive shield above, protecting him.

'I know what it is!' proclaimed Josh. 'I'm in *actual Space Invaders!*'

'Correct, Josh.' The voice from his watch wasn't Tate this time, it was his dad. 'Let's see what you can do.'

Josh soon worked out that both the control sticks did the same thing: simply left, right, and shoot. Josh was ambidextrous, but with computer games he preferred his left hand (as per his immediate reaction), so he used that one.

He remembered that *Space Invaders* was one of the first

arcade games, and one of his dad's favourites as a kid.

'Haha!' laughed Josh, 'I should have known you'd do this, Dad. Maaaaan you're old!'

'Haha!' Cat laughed back. 'We'll see if I'm past it by the end of this, Kidda!'

Josh set about his task. It was simply: destroy all the alien ships before they touch down. At first it was easy, as they moved very slowly. Josh streaked back and forth across the ground, his laser constantly firing and destroying the invaders. Then he utilised a tactic he'd learned from his dad, and settled under one of his shields. He blasted straight up through the middle of it and then he was protected from either side as he destroyed a plethora of silver crab like invaders.

Soon there were only seven left, tightly grouped and moving back and forth, much faster, across the sky. And much lower now.

Then suddenly a large silver flying saucer appeared at the far left, high in the sky. It said 'T.A.T.E' across the hull in lettering almost as big as the ship. And as it flew over Josh it let go a *huge* blast of energy groundwards. Josh *only just* flicked his ship out of the way before it decimated his shield and exploded.

Josh kept moving to the right and fired off a quadruple laser blast. The first three arrived too early, but the fourth hit Tate dead on, after which he promptly exploded into a firework display which read 'Performance Bonus'.

'Well done, Joshua,' was the voice which crackled from his watch this time.

'Hey, Tate! Thanks!'

Josh was really having fun on this one, but he knew there was a job to do. He carefully picked off the remaining ships, as they got faster, and lower. And then there was one left, but it was only about three sweeps across the sky from landing. And moving *very* fast.

Then Dad's voice came from the watch again, 'You won't get me Josh! Haha!'

Josh's eyes hadn't left his target and suddenly he could *actually* see his dad leaning out and waving from the window of the final ship as it sped across the sky, lasers blasting!

Left, right, missed! Right, left, missed! Josh knew he was on his last shot as his ship sped back to the right, just behind the invader. And at the last moment, he was underneath it. *Blam! Kablooooey! Boooooom!* Josh had destroyed his dad's ship the moment before it would have landed – on top of him!

'Arrrrgh. Ya got me!' said Cat-Dad (via the Tate watch). 'Well done, Kidda. On to the next.'

Chapter 28 'Wacka wacka'

ZZZZZZZZZZAP!

Josh was looking down a long hallway, with gold walls. And lots of weird-looking golden globes levitating consecutively in front of him. He took a step forward. He saw a bright yellow 'mouth' close in front of him and heard the strange noise, 'Wacka'.

'What the doof?!' He took three more steps.

'Wacka wacka wacka.' During which his vision was opening and closing with the yellow mouth, and on the last 'wacka' he swallowed one of the globes!

'What the doof, Daddio, I'm Pacman!'

'That's right, Kidda,' his dad replied. 'And I'm comin to get ya! The map is on your watch.'

Josh glanced down at the screen on his watch (it felt a bit weird that it wasn't Tate today). He saw the layout of level 1 on another of his dad's favourite 1980s arcade games, and he knew the route to take, as he had also played it many times at dad's house. Cat-Dad had introduced him to these games before he turned three!

'OK, Josh, let's do it,' said Josh to himself, and soon he was making his way through the maze, gobbling up the 'globes'. He could also see the location of the four ghosts trying to catch him. (In *Pacman* there are four baddies trying to stop you.)

At first, just like *Space Invaders*, it was easy. Easy to avoid the ghosts, and easy to pick up points. And then he found himself approaching a corner, with a ghost right behind him. He glanced over his shoulder and the red ghost had Dad's face! (It wasn't a *scary* ghost, by the way, it was a very funny red blob!) Josh knew that right in the corner was a 'power-up' globe. He reached it just in time, ate it, and turned to face the Daddio ghost, which had now turned blue and was floating away as fast as possible.

'Wacka wacka wacka! Gulp!' Josh had eaten Daddio! (But Dad wasn't too worried about that as there was three more of him, and the fourth would instantly be reborn anyway.)

'Wacka wacka wacka!' Josh continued to make his way through the maze. On his way round he picked up several commendations by eating a giant strawberry, a giant apple, and a giant banana! He also ate Dad twice more after consuming power-ups in another two corners of the puzzle.

As he approached the final corner (top right on his Tate map) he had almost completed the level, but he could see that all four Dad ghosts were closing in on him.

'Wacka wacka wacka.' He sped towards the corner, with a power-up waiting tantalisingly for him. He knew if he got that he would win! But as he made the final approach (the last three 'Wacka's'!) a green ghost dad appeared from the right with a cheeky grin on his face!

'Argh!' Josh exclaimed, and had to immediately turn back. And there was red ghost Dad! Josh ran straight into him.

'Bweee-ooo-eee-ooo-eee-ooo-blurp. Quack quack burp!'

Josh's yellow Pacman mouth folded back and disappeared.

Red ghost Dad transformed into IDF Dad, and he said, 'Better luck next time Kidda!' with a wink.

Josh wasn't pleased. 'Not fair, Dad! It was four to one!'

'It always is in this game, Josh, you know that. And sometimes it is out there, too. Don't sulk! You did great. Ready for part three?'

Josh gathered himself up. He was very competitive, like his dad, and didn't like to lose at anything. Ever! He took a deep breath and said, 'Yeah, Dad, let's go!'

Chapter 29 MI6 or go to the flicks?

ZZZZZZZZZZAP!

Josh found himself in what appeared to be a ventilation shaft. It seemed vaguely familiar. He didn't know why, as he had never before been in a ventilation shaft! He crawled forward, and instinctively took a right turn when he came to a T-junction. A right and a left turn later, he found himself looking downwards from the duct onto a ... toilet!

At this point his Tate watch crackled into life. It was Dad.

'Hey, Kidda. Do you know where you are yet?'

It suddenly dawned on Josh. 'What the doof, Dad? We're in *Goldeneye*!'

Josh was bang on. He had materialised in an *actual* version of a game he had played many many times with his dad on his old Nintendo 64. The game was based on a *James Bond* film. And they were in his dad's favourite level, 'The Facility'.

'OK, Kidda,' said Dad, 'Licence to Kill. Go!' 'Licence to Kill' was the level they always played on. It meant that the slightest nick or wound means *game over*. Dad always said to Josh, 'In reality if you get peppered with fifteen bullets, you can't pick up a health pack and be back to 100 per cent!'

Josh glanced down at what was usually Tate. The screen was showing a map of the area. But no sign of the location of Daddio. He knew The Facility off by heart anyway and now it was time to *move*.

He jumped down from the duct into the toilet cubicle, and without pause ran through the washroom. (He also knew where he would find the best weapon.) As he exited the Gents he lurched to the left, the weapon in sight on the floor. He dove forward through an (expected) hail of gunfire. His dad was on the lower level, hoping to get to him sooner, hoping for a quick kill. (Training kill, of course! In AR training there are no *actual* injuries.)

Josh picked up an RC-P90 fully automatic rifle, and a box of ammunition, and jumped to the left through a pair of double doors as the bullets sprayed around him. 'Not on target, Daddio Mantra!' he laughed.

He wasn't sure whether Dad would try to chase him or cut around the other way through The Facility. He decided that either way, now that he had survived the initial attack, he had the upper hand. He ran forwards, down a steel stairway, and onto the ground floor. He sped along several hallways, passing several *actual* rooms. For a few tense moments, he didn't know whether Dad was in front of him or behind him.

And then he did know. Cat appeared from around a corner at the end of the hallway. Josh was amused to see that his Dad *actually* looked a bit pixelated and appeared to be wearing a low-definition tuxedo! Josh fired without hesitation, and now bullets rained all around Daddio. But he cut back behind the corner again, somehow avoiding getting hit.

As Josh gave chase he glanced down at his arms and weapon, and noticed for the first time that he was *actually* pixelated and tuxedo'd as well!

'Very retro, Daddio!' he laughed. 'I've got you now!'

'It ain't over till it's over, Kidda,' came the radio-link reply.

Josh turned the corner. As he did he spotted a steel

door sliding shut off to his left. He was there in moments, and through into a dimly lit grey room, another door sliding shut now to his right. He got there in time and squeezed through.

Now he saw Cat, about 150 metres ahead running down a much larger hallway, with silver-grey bulkheads, and windows to the left and right. He pounced forwards, once again firing his RC-P90, and once again getting through a steel door before it closed on him. Just as he had Dad in his sights. 'Click.'

'Argh!' said Josh, 'Reload!' He wasn't sure how to do this in *actual Goldeneye*. But as soon as he released the trigger, it did it for him. A gleaming new magazine appeared under the rifle.

However, this had given his Dad time to escape through (another) sliding door to the right. Josh didn't slow down, he knew his dad would be quick to mount a defence. He got to the door, closed this time. He hit the access panel and as soon as it was open enough dived forwards into the room firing to his left. (This was where Dad always went on the N64. It was a huge chamber, with four massive (what appeared to be) gas tanks along its centre. But Dad wasn't to his left ... Dad was behind him!

'Gotcha!' said Cat as he opened fire with his own RCP-90.

Josh swerved from left to right as he ran to the far end of the room. He span to the right to find some cover, and suddenly thought, 'Rocket launcher!' He knew there was one in this room from the game. But as he ran over to where it should be... it wasn't there! A couple of rockets, but no launcher! He had to keep running, as Dad was giving chase, constantly firing. The RCP-90 could fire 90 bullets in 15 seconds.

Josh ran back the length of the hall, passing the gas containers to his right. For a moment his dad had stopped firing. He knew he had to get out of there, or he would be pinned down. A sitting target. So he sprinted back for the door, and managed to find cover behind the protruding entranceway whilst he waited for it to reopen. And then he was through! The sound of machine gun fire chased him all the way.

He knew that if he turned right he'd reach a dead end. So he sprinted back the way he had come. He slid the door closed behind him, *just* before he heard bullets impact on its surface.

'Right,' thought Josh, 'I'm gonna wait here, and pounce on Dad when he comes after me.'

Just as he thought that, he heard a disturbing noise from behind the door. It kinda went: 'Skrik! Pyyyyyowwwwoooooooshhh'. And then from *right* behind the door: '*Booooooooommmmmm!*'

'Oh doof,' said Josh. He tried to move away but the flames from the rocket exploded through the door, and as the furthest flicker licked his ankle, that was it. Game over. D'oh.

His *actual* view sank to the floor. And moments later the previously flaming door slid open, and he was looking up at Daddio.

'"Licence to Kill", Kidda,' said Dad. 'I always got you with the rocket launchers!'

Moments later, Josh's surroundings dissolved, and then he found himself back aboard the IDF *Astron*, sitting again next to his dad on the incredibly impressive-looking bridge.

His immediate reaction was to complain. 'Dad! That wasn't fair! You picked your favourite level!'

Dad Mantra smiled lovingly at him. 'Kidda, you very nearly got me. And out there when you're working for the IDF, don't expect too many of the missions to be any easier. Don't forget, you're still only twelve. And hopefully, Daddio's got a few more good years in him yet!'

At this point Josh relaxed and they both laughed out loud.

Then, a familiar digital voice sounded from the front of the bridge. 'Agreed. You performed admirably, Joshua.'

Josh looked round and saw an almost smiling digital face on the view screen.

'Tate!' he exclaimed.

'Hello,' replied Tate in his perfect digital Queen's English. 'I look forward to our next mission, Joshua. I am most confident of your skills.'

Josh was beaming now, and he turned back to look at his dad.

'OK, Kidda,' said Dad. 'I'll really see you in two weeks, sailing on your next school holiday, I believe?'

'Yeah, Dad!' replied Josh. 'Can't wait!'

ZZZZZZZZZZAP!

ZZZZZZZZZZAP!

And Josh and Dad were gone.

And Josh and Dad were home.

PART VIII

JOURNEY TO THE CENTRE OF THE MOON

Chapter 30 IDF briefing

Location: A large base on Earth's Moon (87007 souls aboard).
Year: 2146.
Josh Projection Age: 27.
Situation: The moon has inexplicably become volcanically active. As this was previously considered to be impossible by Earth's scientists, Headquarters have informed Josh that it can only be the work of the IDE. A huge eruption is going to occur in 24 hours (unbeknownst to the population of both Moonbase Delta and, indeed, Planet Earth). According to IDF forecasts, it will be so big that it will kick the moon out of orbit, causing unmeasurable devastation and decimating all life on Earth.
Mission Objective: Stop it!

Chapter 31 Moonbase Delta

ZZZZZZZZZZAP!

Josh found himself, smartly dressed in a silver-grey all-in-one uniform, in what appeared to be – an arboretum! Probably a kilometre in diameter, there were pathways meandering through, with plants and small trees growing alongside. And an oval lake in the centre, upon which people were gliding along in rowing boats.

A large clear dome was overhead, diamond latticed with strong (titanium, according to Tate) white beams. Through the dome Josh could see an incredible view. The stars, the sun, seemingly setting to the right. And a glorious blue blob off in the distance. The Earth. (Of course, the sun wasn't really setting, as the base was facing Josh's home planet, and bathed in perpetual daylight.)

Couples strolled hand in hand, and some groups of people sat in the grass, relaxing and enjoying conversation. Josh had materialised in the shade (not from the sun, but from a man-made 'sun' high in the dome) under a tree at the Eastern side of what he now knew was called Central Park Delta. He knew this because of the quaint old-fashioned-looking wooden sign conveniently right in front of him!

He decided to take a stroll, as opposed to loitering under the tree, and made his way towards the lake.

'OK, Tate,' he murmured, 'spill the beans.'

As Josh enjoyed the 'sunshine', Tate let him know

what they needed to do. 'Local time 3.15pm Joshua. We have 23 hours 56 minutes to achieve our goal.'

'Which is?'

'We must freeze the core of the moon.'

'What the doof?! How are we going to do that, Tate?!'

'Please calm down Joshua, you are, as ever, overexcitable.'

'Oh,' said Josh, calming himself down as best as possible. 'Apologies, Tate. Please continue.'

As Tate spoke, Josh reached the lake and took a left to walk around it. He loved being near any water. *That* was calming. It made him think of being with his dad.

'On Moonbase Delta, they have tunnelpods. They use these machines to travel below the surface through solid rock, and excavate valuable minerals,' Tate began. 'We must commission one of these. It will enable us to travel to the core, and plant an isotonic charge. This will freeze the core, and prevent the impending eruption.'

Josh was both excited and bewildered. 'OK, Tate. You know I've got to ask. Erm ... what's an isotonic charge?'

'Good question, Joshua, I'm pleased you are inquisitive,' said Tate. 'Isotonic charges are used by ships from Moonbase Delta on missions to Jupiter. They are utilised to freeze huge areas of gases in Jupiter's atmosphere and make it possible to actually land ships in the sky, where there are untold quantities of useful fuels like nitrogen and methane to be gathered.'

Josh could think of one thing to say: 'Wow.'

As Josh strolled north, the glistening lake now on his right, Tate explained that they could collect the isotonic charge en route to the tunnelpod hangar. But that they may well encounter difficulties with Moonbase staff en route.

And then they were at the north shore.

'OK, Tate,' said Josh. 'Show me the route.'

According to Tate's display the passage was directly

ahead. As Josh made his way forward, he glanced back over his shoulder at the beautiful arboretum, knowing that the mission was about to truly begin.

About 50 metres from the doorway, the ground suddenly began to violently shake. 'Moonquake!' came the terrified shout from a nearby occupant of Central Park Delta. And as most people dived to the ground, Josh and one other man ran for the door to 'Access all areas'.

Just as they got there, the stranger fell badly with an 'Arrrgh!'

Josh stopped in his tracks and knelt down to help him. 'It's OK, bud,' he said. 'Let's wait it out.'

The tremor seemed to go on forever, but in fact, it was only about 30 seconds. (29.84 according to Tate).

'Ah! Man, my leg,' said Josh's injured acquaintance. 'It's my ankle. Ouch.'

Josh wasted no time. 'Hey, bud, I'm Joshua. Let's get you to sick bay.'

'Th-thanks man. I'm John. I guess we're both in a hurry, huh?'

'You don't know the half of it,' said Josh as he helped him to his feet.

Chapter 32 The wrong way is the right way

As it turned out, sick bay was in the wrong direction, but not too far, and Josh wasn't about to leave a man in pain. He supported John as he hopped along, during which time Josh avoided any questions about himself and made small talk about how beautiful Central Park Delta was.

Soon enough they arrived at their destination and the doors to sick bay smoothly slid open. Sick bay already had two other injured people inside, and one of the nurses pointed out a bed Josh could plant John onto. It was at the far side of a circular room, with beds around the circumference and consoles and diagnostic tools in the centre. 'They like round stuff on Moonbase Delta,' Josh thought privately. It reminded him of some of the old sci-fi stuff his dad had shown him.

He helped John onto his designated bed, at which point John held his hand and shook it vigorously, saying, 'Thanks, Lieutenant, I really appreciate this.'

At this point Josh learnt his own rank! He hadn't known what the insignia on his uniform meant until now.

'No problem, John,' he replied. 'Gotta get back to it.' And with a final handshake he was on his way.

As Josh made his way to exit sick bay, there was a vibration on his arm. He brought Tate close to his face with a whispered, 'What?'

'On scanning the room I have detected a level 10

security pass on the central console Joshua. It would be most helpful if we can appropriate it.'

'Got ya, Tate,' said Josh.

'Silver. Credit card size,' replied Tate.

The staff in sick bay were far too busy to take a blind bit of notice as Josh discreetly picked up the security pass on his way out and slid it into his pocket.

The doors opened and they were back on track.

Josh carefully followed the route showing on Tate's face, and was relieved to realise that the crew were far too busy rushing around after the quake to look at him, and not recognise him! The isotonic storage facility would be the first stop, before heading down several levels to the subterranean tunnelpod hangar.

Without incident Josh reached his first destination. The security pass didn't open this door. It was met with a 'Barp! Level 12 security required.'

'Doof,' said Josh. But Tate hacked the entrance code within 30 seconds.

The door slid open and they slid inside. They were met with a rectangular (for a change!) brightly lit white room, full of titanium storage units, each shelving four isotonic charges. They glowed a spectacular incandescent sky blue from the centre, with shifting tendrils of light reaching for the outer casing. They were 2 feet wide and 1 foot high, with oval edges.

'What the doof, Tate!' exclaimed Josh. 'I've got to carry one of these undetected?!' Josh was 'doofing' a lot today!

'I'm afraid so, Joshua,' replied Tate. 'We are only 200 metres from the elevator to subterranean level. I will scan for possible interception.'

Josh gathered one of the charges into his arms. He actually had expected it to feel cold, but it didn't, just smooth – and easy to drop! And they prepared.

The moment Tate called the all clear they were through

the door and on the run. Josh's *actual* body was quick, and they soon arrived at the turbolift. Josh quickly stabbed the call button and it was on its way to them. From 1.5 kilometres below!

Josh almost laughed. It was like waiting for a lift at a hotel! Except this was slightly more serious.

'Moonbase Delta staff approaching, Joshua,' stated Tate.

Oh nooooooo! Josh stabbed again at the call button, hoping in vain that it would make the elevator arrive quicker. And then, thankfully, the doors slid open. Josh rushed inside and carefully placed the isotonic charge on the floor. He anchored it to the left-hand side of the chamber with his foot, hoping it would not be seen.

'Level minus 50 Joshua,' said Tate. And Josh had pressed the button before the sentence was complete.

At that precise moment, a Moonbase officer rounded the corner at the end of the corridor, spotted Josh, and quickly waved his hand shouting, 'Hey! Hold the elevator!' Josh faked an attempt at pressing the 'Hold' button, and, heart pounding, shrugged his shoulders in a 'Sorry, too late!' kinda way. And the doors slid shut *just* in time.

Phew!

Josh took a moment to gather himself, and then also gathered the charge back into his arms. It wasn't light, it probably weighed about 15 kilos. Despite it being a 1.5 kilometre journey, the travel period was short, about two minutes. During which time Tate warned Josh that there was a security guard outside the tunnelpod hangar.

'D'oh!' was all Josh could comment on that.

Chapter 33 Frying tonight

The doors of the turbolift swished open and Josh immediately laid eyes on his target, the entrance to the tunnelpod hangar, 25 metres in front of him. And with a young female security guard, *armed*, and wearing a similar uniform to his own, standing in front of the door.

She looked green (that is, new to the job, and not too confident). Josh decided to march with a commanding air about him and supreme confidence. Moments later he was right in front of her.

'S-sir,' she said, looking perturbed. 'Why are you carrying an isotonic charge?'

'*Atten-tion!*' Josh shouted.

The sheepish guard stood immediately to attention, her laser rifle at her side.

Josh knew his authoritative act was working.

'Now listen here, officer. Er ...' he glanced at the name badge on her uniform, 'Fryer. I am under direct orders from Delta HQ to take this charge to the centre of the moon and neutralise all volcanic and tectonic activity. Understand?!'

'Sir! Yes sir!' came the sharp reply. Officer Fryer stood aside and beckoned Josh to stroke his security pass against the panel on the door.

'Gulp!' Josh was relieved that the young security guard hadn't heard that. All the same, he took the silver card out of his pocket (whilst somehow holding the charge with one arm!) and swept it past the sensor.

There was no delay this time, the panel immediately

lit up green whilst a female version of Tate said 'Access granted'. And the door swept open.

Josh looked back at Fryer, feeling a bit sorry for her now, as she seemed a bit overwhelmed. 'Thank you, Fryer,' he said. 'You have served your moon and your planet well. You really don't know how well.'

As Josh stepped through the doorway, officer Fryer beamed back at him. 'Thank you, sir! What's your name? Er, sir!'

As the door slid shut he looked over his shoulder at her and said with a wink, 'It's Josh.'

Now Josh looked forward. He was in an enormous cavern, literally carved out of moonrock, 100 metres high, 100 metres wide, and 500 metres long. Parked along the sides were nine tunnelpods, and one at the far end mounted and facing at an angle downwards on the launch platform. When Josh had heard the word 'pods', he had assumed they would be small. But they were *big*: 200 feet long, and 70 feet high. Dark grey, and with three sets of drill-like teeth at the bow.

Josh knew which one he wanted. Obviously the one on the launch platform and, of course, at the far end of the cavern. And so the sprint was on!

'Go, Joshua,' stated Tate.

There was no time for hiding and sneaking. Josh ran straight down the centre of the cavern. He saw one or two engineering staff working on the pods, but thankfully they were too involved in their work to see him.

And then they were there. A lift in the scaffold was ready to take them up the 50 metres to the rear of the downward-angled pod. Josh was worried that the clunk and clank and buzzing noises it made as they ascended might draw attention, but thankfully they didn't. No doubt the engineers were so used to hearing such noises that they didn't seem out of place.

The elevator clunked to a stop. And moments later, the pod itself let out a *whoosh*. Steam and smoke spread from the sides as the backlit entranceway lowered into position. It was time to go.

Chapter 34 Journey to the centre of the moon

Josh scrambled into the pod and ran downhill (due to the pod's launch mounting angle) to the cockpit. After navigating several chambers, all empty as this pod was readied for the next mining mission, Josh arrived. The pilot's chair was central, right in front of the view screen. He carefully strapped the isotonic charge into the co-pilot's chair, and momentarily had himself strapped in also. At this point, Josh paused.

'Erm ... what now, Tate?'

'The big red button on your control console, Joshua.'

Josh hit it. At that moment huge klaxons began to wail in the cavern outside the pod, and bright red lighting flashed around them. Another female digital 'Tate' voice stated, 'Launch countdown one minute.'

The pod's com system crackled into life seconds later. 'This is an unauthorised launch! Cancel immediately!'

Josh held his *actual* breath as he saw a member of the mining staff run into view below the pod and start punching buttons on a control console.

'They are attempting to lock the mooring anchors, Joshua,' stated Tate. 'I am logging into the main frame.'

The seconds passed, the klaxons wailed, and the countdown continued: '28, 27, 26 ...' And then, *kerchunk!* Another alarm sounded in the cockpit.

The pod's female computer said, 'Mooring anchors locked. Abort launch.'

'Tate?!' said Josh.

'Bear with me, Joshua,' came Tate's ever calm reply. 'I have passed security protocols. Logged in.'

'11, 10, 9 …'

'Tate?!'

'8, 7 …'

Kerchunk! 'Mooring anchors released.'

'6, 5 …'

At this point the man on ground level abandoned his console and began waving frantically at Josh.

'4, 3 …'

Josh saluted him with a wink.

'2, 1 …'

WHOOOOOSSSSHHHH!

They were away! Travelling down the pre-cut launch tunnel and soon, heading straight down.

'Phew!' said Josh. 'I think you do this on purpose, Tate!'

Tate then explained to Josh how they would initially be able to travel down existing tunnels, with the pod using anti-gravity thrusters. 'It can be likened to a train, Joshua, no steering required.' During mining activities, Moonbase Delta teams had travelled to 1000 km deep. 'We will have to tunnel a further 800 km, Joshua. According to my projections we will arrive close enough to the core to deposit the charge two hours and 17 minutes before deadline.'

'Sweet as a nut, Tate!' said Josh as he leant back in his chair and plonked his feet comfortably onto the control console. 'I can chill out now, then!'

'Unfortunately not, Joshua. We will arrive at the rock face in 1 minute 12.76 seconds.'

'Wow! That's a quick 1000 kilometres!'

'Yes, Joshua, and then we have to tunnel.'

They swiftly arrived at the bottom of the pre-cut tunnel, where the pod automatically braked. They were faced with a blank, ragged wall of moon rock.

Josh quickly interpreted how to engage the massive mining drills on their bow and Tate plotted a direct course to the centre of the moon.

Soon the massive engines started, and the even bigger drills began to turn. *Kkkkrrrrnnnnk, buzzzzzzzzz, clank!*

And they were moving again. Through solid rock.

It would be an 18-hour journey, but Josh didn't chill, he made sure he had everything ready. Tate explained to him that the isotonic charge could be set via the pod's launch and delivery system, usually utilised to plant explosives for mining rich mineral deposits.

It was a bit of a faff adapting the launch tube so the charge would fit. And a few 'What the doof?!'s were heard, along with the occasional 'Argh!'

But Josh did it. In six hours.

And then he could relax for a bit, but all the while monitoring the pod's systems as they tunnelled deeper and deeper.

Just as the distance gage read that they were only 50 km from their target depth, a red light flashed up on the console.

'What the doof?' said Josh.

'The indicator states that the secondary gear linkage in drill number three is overheating, Joshua,' said Tate.

'Oh maaaaaaaaan,' said Josh. 'What do we do?'

'I suggest you ready a replacement linkage,' replied Tate. 'They are located in cargo bay one.'

Before Josh left the cockpit he armed the launch system so that the isotonic charge would be fired automatically upon reaching their destination.

And then he was on the move.

He was surprised to find that the linkage was, in fact, just a big cog, about 1 foot in diameter, and 5 inches thick. Tate provided Josh with a map on his screen, and Josh soon found himself in a crawl space, making his way to the drive section for drill number three. Josh had set the onboard computer to give audio updates, so he knew how far they had to go, and what the situation was.

The female 'Tate' said, '18 kilometres to target.' And then, 'Emergency! Overheat in drill number three gear linkage!'

'Yeah, I know that bit,' mumbled Josh as he made his way through the somewhat claustrophobic Jeffries tube.

And then, just after the '5 kilometres to target' update, Josh heard the sound of all the drill engines shutting down. *DWWWwoooooooo. Clonk.*

'Doof!' exclaimed Josh. And he moved even faster.

Very soon he was in the gear linkage compartment. And he immediately spotted the – literally melted – cog. He spotted a huge heavy 'tongue' tool and used it to take the destroyed component off its spindle. And then was ready to put into place the replacement he had lugged through the crawl space. The gear mechanism was against the starboard (right) side of the compartment, and Josh swiftly placed the new cog onto the spindle. But it wouldn't fit in between the larger cogs either side!

'Argh!'

'Time *is* of the essence, Joshua,' stated Tate.

'Tell me something I don't know, Tate!' exclaimed Josh.

Josh lay down on his back, and began slamming at the cog with both feet. It was in place, but wouldn't budge. After a minute of furious stamping ... *click*!

It suddenly slipped perfectly into position.

'Activating,' said Tate.

And Josh heard the engines powering back up, and watched the gear system in front of him start to turn. 'Yes!'

There was no time to get back to the cockpit now, so Josh sat and leant back on the port-side wall, watching his hard work in action, and waiting with bated breath.

'Girl Tate' kept him informed: '4 kilometres, 3, 2, 1 ... Launching charge.'

Soooo matter-of-factly.

Badumph! Phwwwwoooooooom! Booooooooooom!

Moments later Tate spoke up. 'Isotonic charge successfully detonated in the centre of the moon, Joshua. All volcanic activity ceasing. Core temperature, absolute zero.'

'Go on!' smiled Josh. 'How far were we from the deadline?'

'57 minutes, 42.58 seconds, Joshua,' replied Tate.

'Blimey! So we didn't wait till the last minute for once! Ha ha ha!'

Josh felt *incredibly* joyous.

And then the front of the gear linkage compartment began to freeze as the power of the charge continued to spread.

As the ice approached them, Tate said, 'See you next time, Joshua.'

'Can't wait, Tate!' replied Josh.

ZZZZZZZZZZAP!

And Josh was gone.

And Josh was home.

.

PART IX

A 'PITON' THE HAIRY SCARY SIDE

(*piton* – A tool used by mountain climbers to drive into cracks in rock, and attach safety lines.)

Chapter 35 IDF briefing

Location: The peak of the Matterhorn, in the Swiss Alps, Earth.
Year: Now.
Josh Projection Age: 21.
Situation: An Englishman is descending the mountain, after reaching the peak the day before. At some point (as yet unknown) a piton he is using to abseil down 200 metres from a ridge (or buttress) will lose its hold, causing him to fall to his doom.
Mission Objective: Save him!
Additional: Josh underwent two days' training with his dad at IDF Headquarters in preparation for this mission, upon the danger to the climber being forecast.

Chapter 36 On top of the world

ZZZZZZZZZZAP!

Josh materialised in full climbing gear, loaded with all the paraphernalia he needed, ropes aplenty over his shoulder, and two backpacks, including one full of equipment.

He was standing near the edge of the west face of the Matterhorn, surrounded by an incredible spectacle. Blue skies all around, and a few white clouds. *Below* him. He could actually see the curvature of the Earth on the horizon.

'Hmm,' he mused, 'I don't feel cold at all!'

'Good morning, Joshua,' said Tate. 'That is correct. IDF have disabled temperature sensors in your projection, so as not to inhibit your performance on this mission.'

'Sweet!' exclaimed Josh. 'So, any updates on the mission bud?'

'Yes, Joshua, I have scanned for the progress of the climber in need of assistance. His piton will fail in three hours, 27 minutes, 48.76 seconds.'

'OK, Tate, you really don't need to be *that* precise!' said Josh.

'On many occasions, I *have* needed to be Joshua.'

'Er ... OK, Tate, I see what you mean. Doof,' Josh corrected himself.

'At that moment he will be 1.24 kilometres below our current position,' Tate continued, 'so we need to begin our descent immediately.'

'Right, Tate. I'm on it,' replied Josh.

He immediately set about sorting the equipment he needed. Most importantly, a pocket full of pitons and a trusty ice hammer, mounted in a holster on his hip. (Just where he had had a Colt .44 not so long back!)

He took a mental picture of the incredible view. And then he was on his way.

Tate showed Josh the route that the climber had taken, and he was able to follow exactly in his footsteps. This saved a lot of time, as he was able to use the pitons and cams (devices used to clamp into larger cracks in the rock) that had been left behind. Of course, Josh wasn't in any *actual* danger, because if he slipped and fell, IDF would ZZZZAP him out before he crash-landed. This gave him the freedom to proceed without fear, which enabled him to move faster. Josh knew that the man he was there to save *was* in danger, very much so. *Immediate* danger.

Josh totally enjoyed the abseiling part, he descended two 100 metre and one massive 275 metre rock faces in that fashion. He had never *really* abseiled, only in AR training. He had inherited his dad's fear of heights.

On the way he nattered to Tate. 'I might really try this you know, Tate.'

'If you do, Joshua, your training will come in very handy. But please be careful, for you to suffer an injury would be most unhelpful.'

'Heheh! Thanks for your concern, Tate!'

Soon they were only 300 metres above their target height, and came across the most difficult part of the descent yet. Josh had to make his way across a tiny shelf along the rock face, jutting out at the widest part by 2 feet, and at the slimmest part, as little as 10 inches.

'What the doof?!' said Josh.

'37 minutes precisely, Joshua, we must make haste,' replied Tate.

There was no time for attaching safety lines, Josh had to just go for it.

He carefully began to sidestep along the shelf, trying to take no notice of the huge drop behind him. The shelf was about 40 metres long. At the end there was a platform, and safety.

30 metres to go ... 20 ... Small pieces of shale fell away from beneath his feet as he made his way. 10 metres ... 5...

'Argh!'

Josh slipped on some ice, and instantly found himself clinging to the shelf by his fingertips. No time to hesitate. Josh didn't look down, he reached for the ice hammer in its holster with his left hand, whilst clinging on determinedly with his right. He hooked it over the edge of the shelf above him and somehow pulled himself back up. Then he was sitting, with his feet dangling over a 200 metre drop!

'Phew!'

In a few moments, Josh was back on his feet, and completed traversing the hairy, scary shelf.

'23 minutes, 17.97 seconds remaining, Joshua,' was Tate's only comment!

There were some discarded supplies left behind here, where the man Josh was here to save had obviously stopped for a rest and some food.

Josh found the piton left behind by the climber and soon abseiled the 200 metres down to the next ridge.

There was some careful clambering to follow, down some ragged outcrops. And then Josh was on the platform from which the climber had just departed.

Chapter 37 Swing high and fly

'1 minute, 34.56 seconds, Joshua. Danger is immediate. There is only one way we can get to him in time now.'

'Doof! What's that, Tate?!'

'Move 100 metres south, anchor a piton, and swing.'

'What the doof! OK. Tate, I got ya.'

Josh sprinted 100 metres along the rugged outcrop, smashed a piton into the rock, tied on a rope, and attached it to his harness. He then sprinted a further 50 metres away from his target and *jumped*. He knew that he had to jump that way, and then swing back the other way.

Josh twisted in the air so he would be facing the right way, and moments later the rope snapped tight. He swung a bit further to the south, and then like a pendulum began to swing back towards his target. He didn't have time to think about being *Spiderman*, as Tate counted down the seconds. '7, 6, 5, 4 …'

He could see the climber, about 50 metres below him, abseiling down, unaware of the danger.

And then he could *see* it, the piton, hanging dangerously loose, carrying the man's full weight, and *moving*.

Josh had one shot, and one shot only. About two-thirds of the way through his swing, he was *on* it. And as he sped past, he hit with his ice hammer, and smashed the piton deeply and safely back into the crack.

Mission accomplished!

Josh had planned for what happened next.

Just before he reached the top of his swing, Josh released his harness, and was momentarily in *freefall*! *Less than* moments later he had discarded his equipment backpack, and pulled the cord on his second pack.

A parasail was released, and then Josh wasn't falling, he was floating, flying, gloriously soaring through the bright blue sky around the Matterhorn.

'Yessssss!' exclaimed Josh joyously.

'Well done, Joshua,' said Tate. 'A most impressive performance.'

Josh glanced up at his parasail, and saw that it was, in fact, a Union Jack. 'Heheh!' he said, 'Nice one, Daddio!' He knew this would have been his dad's idea, with him being such a *James Bond* fan.

He pulled on the left cord, and swung round to head back past the climber. He glided by, virtually level with him, and the man turned and waved in his harness. He had no idea how close he had came to falling. Josh smiled and waved back knowingly.

Josh didn't immediately dematerialise and head home this time. At his own request, via Tate, he stayed for a while. After all, they were still nearly 3 kilometres up in the air, which was quiet, and the view was spectacular!

He took in the incredible surroundings of the Alps as he floated around the Matterhorn for another two hours.

Then, just as he touched down ...

ZZZZZZZZZZAP!

And Josh was gone.

And Josh was home.

PART X
FUTURE'S PAST (NEMESIS STAGE 2)

Chapter 38

ZZZZZZZZZZAP!

Josh found himself back on the bridge of the IDF *Astron*. He loved to be there, but wondered why he had been called so urgently by his Dad.

After glancing around the bridge, Josh noticed that he had been projected as himself, 12-year-old Josh, and in the exact clothes he had been wearing at home (a scruffy T-shirt, and a pair of jeans).

He had materialised at the back of the bridge, near the turbolift doors, and his dad was waiting for him standing next to the view screen at the front. He was dressed equally casually, in jeans, T-shirt and his trademark bandana.

'Hey, Kidda!' said his dad, as he made his way towards him.

'Hey, Daddio!' replied Josh gleefully.

They met in the middle of the bridge and enjoyed a father–son hug.

Josh was curious. 'So, what's happened, Dad?'

His dad's face took on a more serious demeanour. 'Have a seat, Kidda.'

They sat down, his dad once more in the captain's chair.

'OK. This is where we're at. The IDE have created a temporal vortex and sent Kasabian back in time.'

'Er, OK.' Josh felt a bit flummoxed.

'They've sent him to Doniford, Kidda, the place where

I met your mom. And his mission is to *stop* me meeting your mom.'

'What the doof?!' Josh exclaimed. 'Well, what do we do?!'

'That's why I had to get you here straight away, Josh,' his dad replied. 'To protect you from any changes in the timeline. If Kasabian succeeds, you will never have existed. Their intention is to erase you from IDF history. Obviously they now see you as a threat to their plans.'

Josh felt a bolt of fear. 'Dad! I'm scared!'

'Don't be scared, Kidda, we got you here in time. I need you to be strong now. Your future, *our* future, and our *past*, depends on you.'

'Flippin' 'eck, Daddio,' said Josh. And then repeated himself. 'Well, what do we do?'

'Stay calm, Josh,' said Dad as he grabbed Josh's hand. 'I know you can do this. I'm gonna hand you over to Tate.'

They both looked up at the view screen of the IDF *Astron*, where Tate's digital face looked warmly at Josh. Somehow, knowing Tate was always with him gave Josh that extra bit of belief and confidence.

'Hello, Joshua,' said Tate.

'Hello, Tate,' Josh replied, already feeling better for hearing his voice.

'We cannot triangulate the exact time of Kasabian's arrival in Doniford Bay. However, we can make sure that you arrive before him. You must keep a close eye on everything there. Your mission? Simply to stop Kasabian.'

Josh's first thought came straight out of his mouth. 'Can't you do it, Dad?' he said as he looked up hopefully into his dad's eyes.

'I would have very much preferred to, Kidda,' his dad replied. 'But unfortunately I cannot cross my own timeline even in projected form. If I did, it would cause a temporal paradox of which the consequences would be, let's just say, not too rosy!'

'Doof!' said Josh. But he gathered himself up, looked back at Daddio and said, 'OK, Dad, game on. Let's do this.'

'Lovely jubbly, Kidda,' Cat replied. 'I know you can do it.'

At this conclusion they stood up, and had one more hug for luck.

'See you on the flipside, Kidda!' said Daddio.

'See you very shortly, Joshua,' said Tate.

And ...

ZZZZZZZZZZAP!

Chapter 39 IDF briefing

Location:	Doniford Bay, Somerset, UK, Planet Earth.
Year:	1991.
Situation:	The Inter-Dimensional Empire has sent young operative Kasabian back in time with the intention of creating a future where Josh, for one, doesn't work for the IDF; and for two, doesn't exist! If the plan succeeds, Josh's parents will *never* meet.
Josh Projection Age:	21.
Mission Objective:	Stop Kasabian.

Chapter 40 Back in time

ZZZZZZZZZZAP!

Josh found himself in a small, tidy living room, which he recognised immediately. Simple and clean, there was a sofa, two lounge chairs, a dining table in front of the window, and a TV in one corner, a simple but adequate kitchen in the other.

'G'day Tate! I'm in a chalet!' he said to his watch.

'Yes, Joshua, we have indeed arrived in Doniford, 1991. IDF HQ has calculated that this domicile will not be occupied this week by holidaymakers, so we can use it as a base.'

'Excellent!' Josh replied.

Doniford Bay was, and still is, a holiday park/camp. These institutions are very popular in the UK. Its huge grounds were filled with chalets, such as where they were, and static caravans, also some space for people to bring their own touring caravans, and even pitch a tent. At the centre of the complex are all the amenities anyone could need. A shop, an arcade, a large entertainment complex, a swimming pool and a go-kart track!

Josh looked out of the window onto a sunny day. He had been here once before with his dad. Things were the same as he remembered, and also kinda different.

This of course was due to the fact that it was 1991, and Josh had been there in 2011.

Trying to contemplate that was beginning to give Josh

a headache, so he decided not to! He chuckled, looking at the very old-fashioned but brand new telly in the corner, and left it at that! Josh actually felt really happy to be there, despite the serious implications of his mission.

'OK, Tate,' he said. 'What's the plan?'

'I suggest we locate your father as soon as possible, Joshua,' Tate replied. 'We must maintain surveillance on him and await Kasabian's arrival.'

'Got ya.'

Josh picked up the chalet key, which was placed on the dining table with a welcome note for future guests, and excitedly headed out.

His chalet was located quite high up the hill of the camp, not a steep incline, a gentle stroll either way really. He headed first, as always (and as he knew his dad did too) towards the sea. When he reached the wooden barrier that was in place to stop people tumbling down onto the shale beach he took a left and headed down into camp. It was a doofing beautiful day!

'What month is it, Tate?' he enquired. This weather was extremely awesome for the UK!

'July, Joshua. According to IDF logs, your parents will meet tomorrow.'

'Ah! Well, that explains the weather! And it sounds like we're on schedule.'

As Josh walked down towards the centre of the holiday park his eyes searched the beach for Daddio. It could barely really be classed as a beach. It was shale and a bit of imported sand at first, then rocks, then mud! He had enjoyed scouring the rock pools for sea life with Dad in 2011 so he knew that was a possibility.

No sign, so he continued down, breathing in the salty sea air. He passed the (yes downwards-sloping!) football pitch, the (not-sloping) crazy golf course, and then right after the golf course, he joyously took in the sight of the go-kart track.

It was high season, the camp was full, and the karts were buzzing around the circuit. Josh *loved* karting, he'd been three times with Dad recently: Dad 2-1 Josh. He had won the last one, though, so considered himself reigning champion!

'Tate …' Tate already knew what he was going to say.

'Yes, Joshua, you have funds. Check your back pocket.'

Josh was very pleased to find a small clump of notes. £100 in £10 bills.

'Sweet! Well, it'd be rude not to!'

Josh got straight into the queue. His excuse to himself was whispered. 'You never know, learning this track might be important for the mission.' Yeah, right!

These weren't the fast karts he was used to with Dad. They were designed, obviously, with safety in mind for the holidaymakers. Just a bit of fun in the sun.

Josh quickly learned that he could circle the lap without braking at all. Foot to the floor, pedal to the metal etcetera etcetera. The speed was in the cornering. Basically he lapped everybody on the circuit before the end of the race.

'Ooooooosh!' said Josh to Tate as he strolled away.

'Not your most difficult task to date, Joshua,' Tate replied.

'OK, OK,' said Josh. 'Don't harsh my buzz dude, every win's a win! Haha!'

And every win gets a grin with Josh!

Josh knew his way around the park, and headed towards the clubhouse. Just in front of the rear entrance was the chip shop, and the enticing aroma of the cooking fish (and chips!) found its way to Josh. 'Hmm. Tate, can I eat?' Josh didn't feel hungry, but that smell …!

'Of course, Joshua,' said Tate. 'As you know your projected *actual* body does not require sustenance, but it does mimic all the functions of a *real* human body.'

'Excellent!'

And *then*.

As Josh joined the small queue, there was *Dad*! Right in front of him. With three mates, laughing and joking. He hadn't recognised him at first, but it was *him*! It was really weird to see him there right in front of him, at the age of 23.

Josh tensed up for a moment, not sure how to act. His 23-year-old dad was 2 feet away from him! He felt a vibration on his arm from Tate and thought, OK, just chill. Act normal. What's normal?!

He waited in line behind Dad and his friends. It was so weird listening to a conversation that had happened involving his dad before he was born ... and in fact being a party to it when he laughed along with their jokes!

Daddio and his friends were served their food and Josh was next in line. As Dad walked away he looked straight at Josh and said, 'These chips are bostin', mate!'

Josh just smiled politely, totally frozen to the spot. That was his dad, in 1991, talking to him! And he was used to being called Kidda. Never before, 'mate'!

Josh then ordered himself a portion of fish, chips and mushy peas, and made his way to a bench overlooking the sea to calm down, and eat.

The food did indeed have a calming effect, and after finishing the lot he said to his wrist-bound companion, 'Wow. That was very surreal, Tate.'

'You did well, Joshua,' Tate answered. 'Now we must continue surveillance.'

Josh knew he was right, and the serious aspect of this mission had hit home after *actually* meeting his dad.

It was now around 6 pm, and Josh knew there was no point in going back to the chalet. Soon most people in the camp would be heading to the clubhouse for the evening's entertainment. So that was their destination.

He walked around to the front entrance, where many

families and groups of friends were sitting around tables outside, chatting and enjoying the early evening sunshine. Josh made his way into the pool bar (not the swimming pool, the 'shooting pool' bar). All the while keeping his eyes peeled for Dad, Mom and, of course, Kasabian.

The problem with spotting Kasabian of course being, he had no idea of what age he would be projected by the IDE. He had seen some profiles with Dad, so at least he had some idea of what possibilities to look for.

He went to the bar, ordered a cola, and had a wander around the entertainment complex.

With no sightings, he played a couple of games of pool (lost one, won one) and then popped into the arcade. 'It's re-con, Tate!' he exclaimed whilst pumping a few 10 pence pieces into various machines. (He *actually* played several games of *Pacman* just in case there might be a rematch with 'Ghost dad' at IDF!)

At 8 pm, he headed into the main entertainment room of the clubhouse. It held 1000 people, and was where all the action was at night. Cabaret stars, games, and so on. He enjoyed the entertainment, whilst still being 'on patrol', and trying, of course, to blend in.

The rest of the night went like this.

> 8.17 pm:
> There was his mom! At the bar with his beloved granny and grampy.
> This was a moving moment, to see not only his mom age 25, but also his granny and, especially, his grampy. He had passed on the year before, so to see him alive again, and so happy, almost brought an *actual* tear to Josh's eye.
>
> 8.47 pm:
> Josh's dad Cat and his mates arrived in the pool

room, where they stayed for two hours playing pool, laughing a lot, and causing general mayhem and disruption!

11.33 pm:
Josh had prime position at the bar in the main hall, where he could see both his parents, sitting quite a way from each other, enjoying the show. No sign of Kasabian.

12.17 am:
A very pretty (and somewhat inebriated) young lady got chatting to Josh at the bar. He was very flattered, but he had to focus on the mission. And, she was *really* ten years older than him!

01.35 am:
Josh's dad got on stage and sang a karaoke number, 'Fly me to the moon' (originally by Frank Sinatra). Josh noticed that at that moment, his mom noticed his dad.

02.00 am:
Closing time.
There was no interaction, and no further incidents of note. Josh discreetly followed his dad back to his chalet, and noted where it was: only about 200 yards from Chalet 107, Josh's chalet. As they passed, Tate pointed out Cat's car, a 1986 1275GT Mini.

'Ah!' exclaimed Josh. 'Dad told me about that one! I've only seen it in old pictures.'

They got back, and Josh *actually* slept.

Chapter 41 A bit X-iting!

Tate beeped Josh awake at 9 am, knowing full well that this would be before Cat was moving.

Josh scratched his *actual* head, stretched, and immediately noticed his projected pyjamas were replaced with a cool pair of blue jeans, and a Red Hot Chili Peppers T-shirt.

'Tate! How did you know?!' smiled Josh.

'This band were very big in 1991, Joshua, according to IDF logs.'

'Haha!' laughed Josh. 'Perfect.'

Josh poured a glass of water, just because it felt normal to have a drink first thing, and sat at the dining table. Where he had a clear view of Dad's chalet and car. It was another gloriously sunny morning, enough to put a smile on anyone's face.

And then a weird feeling happened. Josh thought for a moment, and dismissed it, thinking, 'Naah. Not possible.'

And then it happened again. And soon it became a constant nagging feeling.

He had no choice but to speak up.

'Erm, Tate …'

'Yes Joshua?'

'Why do I feel like I need a poo?!'

'As I said to you yesterday Joshua, you can eat, and your *actual* body mimics all the functions of a *real* body. What goes in, must come out.'

'Doof!'

And so, Josh went to the loo! And he was *actually* laughing. 'Haha! Of course! It can't just disappear! Haha!'

But no sooner were his ablutions done than there was an alert from Tate.

'Sensors indicate your father is on the move, Joshua.'

'Right. Let's go.'

Josh was straight out of the door (after washing his *actual* hands), and saw that his dad and friends were getting in the car.

'What the doof, Tate?! I can't follow them!'

'Calm down, Joshua. Yes you can. See the red one, parked opposite your father's?'

And there, the other side of the road, was a gleaming '91 plate, Ford Escort XR3i.

'What?! That's mine?'

'Yes, Joshua. Please make haste.'

As Josh ran over to the car, his dad was reversing out of his space. Josh opened the door and jumped in. The key was already in the ignition. He immediately started the car up, and noticed gratefully that it had automatic transmission. He hadn't yet learned how to use a manual gearbox, or as they say in the United States, 'stick shift'. Automatic gearboxes Josh could use, just like with the go-karts: one pedal for go, one pedal for stop.

Josh put the gear lever into 'Drive', released the handbrake, and gently rolled out of his parking space, took a right turn, and was right behind his dad.

'Keep your distance, Joshua,' said Tate.

'Oh yeah!' said Josh, and he braked a bit to give Daddio some distance.

They exited the holiday park, and began to make their way along the beautiful Somerset coastline. Josh recognised the route and guessed correctly that his dad was heading towards Minehead (about 9 miles from Doniford).

Josh felt a bit blinded by the sun a couple of times and said, 'Shades, Tate?'

Immediately a very cool pair of sunglasses materialised with a little 'ZZAP!' on Josh's face.

And whilst they travelled Tate explained the intricacies of the projection of the very snazzy car Josh was driving. 'IDF can only maintain the projection of something of this size for a short time Joshua.'

'How short?'

'24 hours maximum.'

'Well, Tate, let's hope that's enough.'

And then, having just driven along the stunning Blue Anchor Beach, and up through some country lanes, Josh *lost dad*!

His dad was zipping along in the little Mini, and at a junction, got out just before a long trail of traffic trailing behind a tractor.

'Doof!'

Josh had no choice but to wait. And wait he did. It was nearly two minutes before he could resume the chase. And now, on a single carriageway, no chance to overtake. Tate kept track of Daddio's position as they crept along, and thankfully noted that Dad had parked up ahead of them.

Another long two minutes later, Josh caught sight of his dad's car, parked up on the right-hand side of the road about 300 metres ahead. There was a man standing next to it. About 21, in shorts and a black vest. (tank top in US terms).

The man glanced left and then right, before bending down towards the rear wheel of Dad's car. And Josh knew the face. *Kasabian*!

Josh had to throw caution to the wind now, and pulled out of the slow traffic. The other side of the road was clear, so Josh put his foot down and accelerated towards Kasabian.

As he did this he saw his nemesis push a screwdriver into his dad's rear tyre and puncture it. Kasabian looked up and saw Josh racing towards him.

He bolted towards a gleaming black car, the same as Josh's, parked behind his dad's but facing the other way, and jumped in.

'You're not getting away from me, Kasabian,' Josh whispered.

But Josh was moving fast in the wrong direction. He knew there was only one thing to do right now, something he'd learned on his PlayStation. *Handbrake turn!*

He wrenched the handbrake on to 'Full', twisted the steering wheel clockwise, and perfectly span the car around as it skidded to a halt.

Kasabian was just pulling out about 200 metres in front of him.

The chase. Was on.

Josh had his foot on the gas before Kasabian, and as the black XR3i in front of him got up to speed, Josh was right on his tail.

They reached speeds of 120 miles per hour on the straight road back out of Minehead. Tate noted to Josh that there was no danger to other road users. Upon collision, either Kasabian or Josh would simply be BLAAPPED or ZZAPPED out of there with no contact. But Josh couldn't afford to make a mistake. He *had* to catch Kasabian.

Kasabian swung a left, into the country lanes on the way back to Doniford, all the time with Josh right on him.

Then Kasabian bore right. He had no time to check his route, he was just trying to lose Josh. Then they went over a canal bridge, both cars took to the air as if on a stunt jump, then regained their grip on the road.

Soon there was nothing but green fields either side. Josh saw that they were heading towards a T-junction, but at the last moment Kasabian swung a right just before it into an even slimmer country lane. They sped uphill, over the peak, and down the other side. It was a dead end! Just a farmers gate, leading into another field.

Kasabian attempted a handbrake manoeuvre just as Josh had achieved a few minutes ago. But as his car slid around, it hit a bump in the road and flew into the air, turning and landing upside down, sideways on to the approaching Josh.

It skidded on its roof and sparks flew for about 150 metres, and then came to a smoking halt.

Josh pulled up only 10 metres away. And just as he opened his car door ...

BLLLLLLLLLLLAP!

The Black XR3i, and Kasabian, were gone.

Josh got out of his car, and leant on the roof, taking an *actual* breath for a moment. He looked at where Kasabian's car had been just a moment ago. There were scrape marks on the tarmac, but aside from that, it was as if it had never happened.

'Flippin' 'eck, Tate,' he said. 'That was intense. I saw Kasabian puncture Dad's tyre. What's happened now?'

'Excellent performance, Joshua.' Tate replied. 'Kasabian has succeeded in preventing your parents meeting today as *should* have happened. However, the timeline according to IDF HQ indicates that they will *still* meet at some point this week. IDE will not have the power to send something as large as another car in that time, but they *will* have the power to send Kasabian back. I suggest we head back to Doniford, and continue surveillance.'

'Gotcha, Tate.'

As Josh drove back to camp, at a much more mellow pace, he couldn't help but feel irritated that a stupid tractor had stopped him from preventing Kasabian's success.

However, he at the same time felt exhilarated that he had caught Kasabian and stopped him from doing further damage. (For the time being.)

Taking in the view of the beautiful blue sky, and equally stunning blue sea on the way, helped him to relax.

Soon they arrived back at Doniford Bay, and trundled gently into the park. It warmed Josh's heart to see so many happy people. Kids playing football, moms sunbathing, dads cooking on the barbie!

Josh parked the car up, tapped it as he locked up, and said, 'Well done Ford Escort.' He had a habit of talking to inanimate objects occasionally, just like his dad.

That night, whilst no one could see, Josh's XR3i left with a quiet ZZZZZAP.

For the next three days, Josh had to keep a close eye on both his mom and his dad, whilst keeping watch for Kasabian's return. This was a tough job to do, especially without being noticed! His dad spent a lot of time at the pool with his friends, just hanging about, having a splash, and generally having fun. Josh made acquaintances with a few people. That helped. His cover story was that he was a trainee journalist doing a report on holiday camp life for a local paper. Obviously he avoided direct contact with either of his parents. That could only serve to complicate the timeline.

Josh was quite pleased to note that, over the three days, he was getting an *actual* suntan! Tate was quick to remind him that it wouldn't be there when he got back home. 'Doof!' was Josh's first comment on that. 'Well, I guess Mom would wonder. I could have said I got a spray tan!'

There was no sign of Kasabian during this time, and no contact between Josh's parents. As the days passed, Josh's worry increased. Time was running out.

Chapter 42 The final countdown

Josh awoke to Tate's beep at 9 am. This was the final day of his parents' holiday. He had to look out for Kasabian, and somehow hope they would meet, or this was it, end game.

The day started overcast, but soon the sunshine burnt through. Josh did his ablutions (he had enjoyed fish and chips most evenings!), and sat by the window to chat to Tate.

'This is it, Tate. I've got to be honest, I'm scared.'

'You must not focus on that, Joshua,' replied Tate. 'It will impair your performance. Try not to think of it. Focus on every moment and stay sharp.'

Josh sighed, looked down at his *actual* body for a moment, and then took in a deep breath. 'You're right as always of course, Tate. Today is *the* day.'

Ten minutes later Josh saw his dad and friends step out of their chalet, not dressed in swimming pool attire today, but in jeans and T-shirts. Josh was most relieved that they didn't get into Dad's car, but strolled down towards the camp hub.

He was immediately out of the door and following discreetly.

Cat made straight for the Go-Kart track, and got in the queue. Josh lingered for a moment, then whispered to Tate, 'Well, I might as well go for it too.'

As he joined the queue a kid of what looked like Josh's real age (12) slipped in between Josh and his dad.

Josh glanced around the circuit, looking at the cars and the spectators. Oh! There was his *mom*! Watching with Granny and Gramps. At that moment Josh felt a vibration on his wrist from Tate.

Josh held his 'watch' up to his ear. 'Joshua. IDF logs indicate that historically your dad wins this race. If that occurs, projections indicate that your parents will meet during the celebrations, and the timeline will be safe.'

Josh didn't reply, it didn't seem prudent for the people around to see him talking to his watch!

And then.

The kid in front turned around and winked at Josh. It was *Kasabian*!

He had chosen a younger projection age to be lighter in the kart!

'Doof,' thought Josh.

And the next race, they were on.

There were ten karts. Three lads of about Daddio's age got in first, then it was Dad, his three friends, Kasabian, Josh, and a rather portly fellow squeezed into kart number 10.

As they lined up in the pit lane, Josh felt a burst of adrenalin. He knew that *this* was the moment. It could be the last thing he ever did – or *never* did if he failed.

And then they were *off*!

The acceleration on these karts was very underwhelming after the chase a few days ago, but equally important.

By the end of the first lap, Dad had already passed the three cars who started ahead, Kasabian was up to fourth, and Josh had literally followed his tracks into fifth, matching him move for move, and turn for turn.

There was no one on the track who could match Cat,

Josh or Kasabian. The difference was that Cat was racing for fun, and Josh was racing for his *life*.

By lap three the three of them were out in front. And two laps later, they began to encounter traffic as they lapped the slower karts.

This was where Kasabian was able to get right on Dad's back bumper. He touched Dad's kart on a couple of tight corners but couldn't get past.

And *then*.

With two laps to go, Kasabian suddenly swerved out of the way and braked. Josh had no time to react and sped past him, getting closer to Cat. He had no time to even wonder what Kasabian's plan was.

He stayed tight on his Dad's tail. It was the best he could do to keep up!

And as they entered the last lap Josh saw that Kasabian was now just in front of Dad, having slowed down. Then Josh knew what Kasabian was up to.

He planned to take Cat out of the race.

As they headed down the straight towards the final turn, Josh used the 'tow' from Dad's wake to get alongside, but he knew he had no chance of making the hairpin corner from his position in the track.

As they were only feet away from the sharp right, Kasabian pulled in front of Dad. Dad had no choice but to brake. Josh swerved to the left in front of Dad, *banzooka'd* the back of Kasabian's kart at full speed (about 25 mph!), and both Kasabian and Josh span into the rubber side hoarding. Dad cut back to the right, accelerated out of the hairpin, and took the chequered flag!

'*Yesssssssssssssss!*' shouted Josh!

He waited for Kasabian to get his kart turned around, and

followed him over the finish line. He was not letting this guy out of his sight!

They still 'officially' finished second and third having lapped everyone else, but that mattered nothing to Josh, of course.

They pulled up into the pit lane, and exited their karts. Josh put his arm tightly around Kasabian, and escorted him to the side of the kart track booking office. Kasabian struggled valiantly for a moment, and then slouched in defeat, knowing that his 12-year-old projection was no match for Josh at 21.
Josh looked into the eyes of his nemesis. Kasabian didn't look too happy.
And then he glanced out towards the track. His dad had been bouncing joyfully and chatting to his friends. (They didn't do too bad, fourth, fifth, seventh!)
And *then*. He leant on the barrier separating the spectators, took his helmet off, and said to Trina, Josh's mom, 'Allo!'
She looked straight back into his eyes and blushed, and said very politely with a smile, 'Hello.'
They began to chat, and Josh saw his dad shake his beloved grampy's hand.
Tate beeped and said, 'Mission successful, Joshua. The timeline is safe.'
Josh felt like once again shouting '*Yesssssssssssss!*', but he didn't.
He just turned back to Kasabian, and said with a wink, 'Got ya.'

BLLLLLLLLLLAP!

And Kasabian was gone.

And Kasabian was home.

ZZZZZZZZZZAP!

And Josh was gone.

And Josh was home.

Two days later, Josh was sailing with his dad. *Really* sailing with his dad.

THE END

JOSH MANTRA WILL RETURN